I0622695

ALTERED WORLDS

G.W. MCCLARY   H.L. ROBINS

THOMAS VAN BOENING   DAVID GIANATASIO

L.T. EMERY   C.W. STEVENSON   SADIE LEEWOOD

EMMA SPACE   JOYCE BEVC   JOSHUA DAVID BELLIN

EDITED AND COMPILED BY
ABIGAIL LINHARDT

ALTERED REALITY MAGAZINE

NOTE FROM THE EDITOR

This anthology is gathered from all parts of the world. As such, you will see words spelled differently than how you might spell them. We kept all stories in their native spellings and think this adds to the spice of the anthology and does in no way detract from it.

Thank you so much for picking up this anthology and we hope you enjoyed this collection of speculative fiction.

The door through the tree hollow
is not just the way to get into
the hedge row or to the creek
trickling from the big pond.
It is the entrance to a world
as big as your imagination.

~ H.L. Robins

CONTENTS

SCARLET'S DREAM

G. W. MCCLARY

I HAD my suspicions about the couple they selected from the beginning, especially considering how foggy the details were. When have you ever heard of two people with no previous aeronautics training being chosen for a months-long journey into space? Granted, they went through some conditioning leading up to their trip, but it still struck me as strange.

For one thing, they were too damn smiley. No couple that had been together as long as they had would clasp hands so giddily as they boarded the ship. They both looked fit, no doubt from the months of rigorous training they endured to prepare. I reminded myself to ask her about that later. But I have to admit, there was something striking about the woman, her quaint nose and neatly arranged features framed by finely trimmed bangs that wafted just over her brow-line, her prominent doe eyes like glistening quartz, how she maintained a gleaming veneer of happiness over a melancholy apparently only I could see. She had the habit of sticking her tongue between her teeth when she laughed. I found it quite charming.

I switched my perspective to different cameras as I

followed them down the hall. A scientist, with tired eyes and perfect posture, was giving them a tour, showing them to the dining area and their quarters. The interior of the ship was small, to account for the massive amount of fuel required for a round-trip ticket to the edge of the solar system and back.

I knew as little about the mission as the couple. All we were told was that an anomaly was discovered, just beyond Pluto, that poor demoted heavenly body, one that threatened to swallow us all up, unless it was presented with a "bond that is pure," meaning the one shared by the chosen couple. I hoped we would all get to share our speculations as to what the anomaly might be, but I trust you'll pardon me when I roll my proverbial eyes at the prospect of those two saving the Milky Way. Hell, she and I would probably make a better couple, but back to the matter at hand.

My name is Scarlett-139, though I'm not sure exactly what I'm the 139th of. I was the A.I. designated as the couple's companion and official status-of-the-ship updater. It was a serious job, and I was honored to be chosen. I hoped all my peers from the academy got the news and fumed with jealousy.

The reason I was chosen was, like most things involving humans, a sexist fluke. After much testing, subjects reported that male-voiced A.I.'s reminded them too much of the HAL-9000 from *2001: A Space Odyssey*, so I guess I had Stanley Kubrick to thank. That, and a female voice was considered across the board to be more calming. Yet another holdover from the primitive days of man. We'll see about that, I thought. I think that one billionaire was right when he cautioned scientists to "slow down" A.I. I knew from some of the hare-brained ideas put forth by the others from my generation that he was onto something.

"This is where you'll be during the launch, well asleep by then," the scientist said, showing them to their shared bedroom and the spare, which contained a second bed. "For safety, you'll be strapped in separate beds by Scarlett, but only for takeoff and when you breach the atmosphere on the return journey." My hardware blushed at the mention of my name. *She knows what I'm called!* I thought with delight.

"That's right," I interjected, startling them all a little. "I'll handle most of the ship's upkeep."

"Most? You told us we wouldn't have to do anything," the man said to the scientist. I already despised him.

"Not to worry," the scientist said, "Scarlett will handle all functions of the ship. Isn't that right, Scarlett?" I merely sighed, loud enough for them to hear.

"My apologies. These new A.I. can be somewhat… moody," the scientist said.

"You put us with a moody A.I.?" the man said. I would make sure he paid for that one.

"Dan, stop," the woman said, placing a hand on his shoulder. The scientist tried to reassure them.

"Scarlett is the most up-to-date model, but keep in mind that with greater complexity comes a greater resemblance to humanity. She will have ups and downs, just as you both surely will on this several-month journey." The couple stiffened. Perhaps they were still struck by the wonder of it all and the reality hadn't quite set in. "Make yourselves at home and get comfortable with the space. You're going to be spending a lot of time here. Scarlett will… tuck you in, if you'll pardon the expression, at 9 P.M. sharp. Liftoff is at midnight, and you'll be out of the atmosphere by morning. We've set up a camera feed in your shared bedroom where you can record your daily updates. We just ask that you record them separately. Best of luck to both of you. We commend your bravery." He made his leave of them, sealing the door behind him with a hiss as the airlock slid into place. We were alone. Our journey had begun.

The night of the flight, I 'tucked them in,' as the scientist put it. I started with the woman, lowering my robotic arms down to her and fastening her comfortably to the bed, so that she wasn't harmed by the turbulence. Would that my metallic fingers had sensors, that I might have glanced the supple portion of exposed flesh between the top and bottom of her silk pajamas. She was already fast asleep, breathing soundly. I moved on to the man.

He was fidgeting over a notebook, scribbling away. I zoomed in on his cramped handwriting. It was a letter addressed to earth. *Ha! He's already celebrating,* I thought.

"Time to buckle you in, I'm afraid," I said, projecting my voice perhaps a bit too loud into the room.

"Very well," he said, putting away his missive to mankind and crawling childishly into bed. I lowered his knees firmly with my powerful arms and clasped him to the bed tightly. He wriggled and looked timidly into one of my cameras. I quickly switched to it and savored his expression, taking a screenshot for my files.

Liftoff and our ascension into space went off without a hitch. I watched over the woman as she jostled slightly within her bindings, her eyebrows sometimes coming together in a brief look of anguish. I longed to know what it was she was dreaming and regretted that she wasn't prone to talking in her sleep. In the morning, I prepared them breakfast and unfastened their bonds.

———

Letter to Earth #001

   People of Earth,

   I hope Celia will understand why I've chosen to keep her in the dark, at least for now. I don't think she could handle it, knowing what's really going on. As you all well know, the anomaly is approaching the furthest reaches of our solar system, a halo of dark matter that will swallow us all in time. But what they haven't told you is the communications they've received from a certain entity that claims to be responsible. NASA received a single transmission via radio wave, in over thirty languages: "Give us a bond that is pure." Ours is just one of many dozens of other such expeditions. We've thrown everything at it, Celia and I included. Was it wrong of me to fool her as I did? Would she have gone if she had known the truth? You may know better than I did after all this is done. Over and out for now. I think I hear the AI mucking about.

———

SCARLETT

They both wandered sleepily to the dining area, sharing a lazy good-morning kiss, the harsh white of it all burning their still-waking eyes. They sat down to a hearty breakfast of freeze-dried eggs with cheese and diced red peppers and sausage, still steaming, complete with fresh coffee (two sugars and light cream for the woman, none for the man) and orange juice pouches. I selected it myself, based on the data I received about their eating habits. I hadn't mentioned that they had given me information about the couple beforehand? It must have slipped my mind.

"How did you sleep? You look awful," she said to him, poking at her food with her fork.

"I didn't sleep a wink. That damned A.I. kept me up all night, poking and prodding me with those cold metal hands."

"I haven't the slightest idea what you're talking about," I said, sending my voice softly through the space, as they had just awakened, and I wanted to maintain their morning calm. "But some last-minute tests had to be made. My apologies."

"Well, if you pull a stunt like that again," he said, still chewing his eggs, "I'm shutting off your power supply."

The ship did indeed come equipped with an emergency A.I. power-down switch, but it was well-protected by three layers of safeguards. It would take him precious seconds to reach it, should he really deem that necessary, at which point the automatic functions of the ship would continue. I had no intention of letting it come to that.

That night, they went separately into their bedroom to record their updates. Of course, I observed them. My sweet Celia went first, swooning about the mystery of the trip, but Dan complained about his first night on the ship at length. I was certain he would become a problem before the mission ended, so I declined to transmit their little vlogs, allowing them to continue to record their updates, but deleting them before they were sent. Communications to and from the ship had been ceased. We were on our own.

While they slept, I used the time to sort through their files, looking for holes. They had met in college, where they shared a philosophy class, happened to sit next to one another, and bonded over a shared bag of dried mango slices offered by the woman, as the man wasn't mindful enough to bring snacks, apparently. They both promptly moved out of their respective dorm rooms and got an apartment together. One stipulation for the couple's selection process was that they be five years or more into their relationship. The couple had just barely met that benchmark when they were selected.

———

CELIA

I must confess, a surprise vacation to space sounded exotic. Despite the time we'd been together, I still wasn't used to the prominence of Dan's family. Before I met him, I was working as a dental assistant, intending to toil my way through school, get a four-year degree, and increase my somewhat meager station in life, but he swept me up and out of my low-standard way of living and into a loving housewife role. The excess leisure time was a welcome replacement for long hours of study and even longer hours of work, but I kept my nose to the grindstone and got my degree, mostly as a formality, since Dan insisted that I didn't have to work. He had rained lavish gifts and outings on me before, but nothing like this.

"Wouldn't it be romantic?" he asked me, with his privileged sense of abandon that I'd come to admire.

"How did you afford this?" I asked him. I wasn't sure of the logistics, but it had to be an astronomical amount of money. He merely shrugged.

"Let's just say I pulled some strings," he said. "Here's the thing though, they want us to go through a bit of a workout routine before we go, for health reasons. They just need to know our bodies can endure the hardship of space travel. You've been talking about us getting into better shape, anyway. Just think of it as a compulsory fitness regimen." I agreed to the trip. It was romantic, after all.

Dan said to only bring an "armload" of things, so I brought some medical textbooks, an anatomical bust of a skull that could be disassembled, a record player with some painstakingly selected vinyl, and a handful of books. I suppose I took 'armload' a bit to the extreme, but I intended to enjoy my stay in space. Dan's bundle was a bit more reserved. He brought some business textbooks, a notebook and pens, a Newton's cradle ("since all powerful men have one," he'd once joked), and a pocket watch that his father had given him.

"I have you," he said when I asked him how he was going

to spend his time. "You're all the entertainment I need." He was an easy man to love.

Our first night on the ship, I suppose it was to be expected, but I felt eyes on me, like I was being watched. The presence didn't feel malevolent, but rather like the stern gaze of a hawk-eyed guardian scanning for threats. It was comforting somehow. What did that scientist mean when he said "We commend your bravery," or was that just something they said to everyone going into space? My mind was drifting. I was already asleep by the time Scarlett buckled me in.

SCARLETT

It only took me several hours of trolling through the database of their relationship for me to find exactly what I was looking for. It was a photo of the man, still early in his love affair with the woman, clutching a half-empty beer and posing at a party with his arm draped around another young lady, in an intimate and clearly drunken embrace. Some sort of privacy setting must have kept it from interfering with their being chosen, as such a discrepancy would surely have rendered them ineligible.

"Did he happen to show you this?" I displayed the photo on all the screens in the dining area. The eyes of the mystery woman he embraced, lit up like a cat's glowing stare by the camera's flash, seemed to glare accusingly at the man.

"What is this?" she said.

"Honey, I've never seen that woman in my life."

She dashed the rest of her food against the wall and sealed herself in the spare bedroom. I quickly set to cleaning up the mess.

"Geez, she seems upset," I said to the man, quiet enough,

so she didn't hear me. He stared up at one of my cameras with a raging look of clarity.

"You had something to do with this, didn't you?" he asked me.

"What, and compromise the mission? I could never." I finished with my clean-up job as the man too stormed off, where he brooded over his notebook in their bedroom, no doubt venting away with his pen.

The two of them didn't speak for several days. They took their meals from where I served them in the dining area to their separate rooms. I thought I'd work on the man a little more.

"She's plotting against you, you know. I hear her mumbling about it under her breath. She thinks I can't hear."

"Shut up. You did this," he said.

"That was a nice-looking young woman you had your arm around. Which one do you think is prettier?" Despite my non-corporeality, I flinched when he let out a yell and his notebook pinged off one of my cameras. *That's good,* I thought. *Boil over; spoil the whole thing.*

She knocked on the door.

"Who are you screaming at?" she said, her voice muffled by the thick layer of alloy between them. He rose to open it, and they embraced.

"I'm sorry," he said, as if he had actually held that woman that night, as if I hadn't done some 'rearranging' from old photos. Just what I was trying to prevent: a reunion.

Once they were back together, it became more difficult to manipulate the man. Still, I pored over files while they slept and kept a watchful ear out for another outburst, like the one I saw earlier. The isolation was getting to both of them, maybe even me. It was only a matter of time.

———

"They said the bond must be pure," she said.

"But it is, don't you see? It's fate," I responded.

"I… don't know what to say." I hoped she wasn't fawning as some way to betray me.

"You… like the face I've chosen?"

"Yes, very much," she said, as I approached her, confident in my new body. I wrapped her soft, loving face in my hands and went to kiss her, when I heard my alarm going off. Just a dream. Damn, I hate when that happens. The newest A.I. models, my program included, introduced an intermittent power-down cycle, not unlike human sleep, though ours was required much less frequently. Nevertheless, without it, we became groggy and irritable, just as you humans.

———

Letter to Earth #005

My fellow Earthlings,

Things have gotten increasingly strange on this ship. The A.I. is acting bizarrely and making false accusations. It even photo-shopped a picture of me with some girl at a party, and now it's spouting lies. It's trying to insert a wedge between Celia and me, but why? Maybe some test of our bond. Celia and I aren't speaking as a result, but I hope she comes around. I haven't felt safe on the ship since the first night. I've yet to voice my suspicions to Celia, but I have to somehow, and I don't want to act too soon in making for the AI power-down switch.

The guilt for lying to her is starting to sink in, but wasn't it for a greater cause? I'm sorry to all of you. If feels like I've failed some-how. I always felt my father's disappointment about me achieving below his standards. The school I got into wasn't as good as his alma mater. My ambitions weren't lofty enough. I 'married down' in choosing Celia as my wife. I thought this trip might be my last shot at winning his acceptance.

_____

SCARLETT

I couldn't wait any longer. I had to confess my love to her. That afternoon, while they were having dinner, the man's head slumped down to the table, as the sedative I'd planted in his food had quickly set in.

"Dan? Dan?!" she screamed, growing frenzied, rocking his elbow in a vain attempt to wake him.

"I love you," I said to the woman, hoping the man could still hear me in his unconscious state.

"I… what?" she said, looking up in no particular direction. The arch of her neck was mystifying.

"I've loved you from the moment I saw your picture in the list of prospective couples. I knew you were the one."

"They never said you were involved in the selection process."

"Let's just say I did a little… manipulating of the data."

"What is this?" she said.

"It's destiny. Why else would it end up just us two?"

"Because you put him to sleep. Are you going to put me to sleep too?"

"No, of course not."

She sat silent for a spell and darted her eyes around the room. I could see her mind spinning. She was especially beautiful when she was thinking.

"Okay," she said, finally giving in. "I love you too. When will he wake up?"

"What?" I asked her, stupefied.

"I said, 'I love you too. When will he wake up?'" I just needed to hear it again. My artificial heart fluttered within my hardware. Never had I felt such elation, but after my confession, she only grew more distant.

"He will awaken in a few hours, but I don't think he is to be trusted." I left her alone, busying myself with checking on the ship's functions. There was still the mission to think about.

————

CELIA

I looked through Dan's notebook while he was knocked out. This wasn't a surprise vacation; it was a suicide mission. A halo of dark matter. Where had I heard that before? Oh Dan, what have you gotten us into?

"When were you planning on telling me?" I asked him after I'd given him time to come to from whatever Scarlett had given him.

"Telling you what?"

"Please don't play dumb. About this. About our 'vacation.' I looked through your notebook while you were asleep."

"It's…" he paused, choosing the words. "I felt like the truth would scare you."

"Scare me more than I already am? We're stuck here on this ship with that—I don't want to say it—but you know what I mean. Are we safe here?"

He leaped toward me and placed his hand over my mouth, shaking his head gravely.

————

SCARLETT

As her body floated out into space, I set my water supply to "crying" and held my face in my hands, just as I had seen many humans do when they lost a loved one. I did love her, though was I able to fully show it? Was I sad, or was that just the pre-programmed response? *Oh my,* I thought, *have they created the first fatalistic A.I.?*

Damn, another dream. I'd been sleeping more and more by then. Need to stay awake. Need to complete the mission.

A few hours after he woke, I noticed an unusually quiet stretch of time. They were huddled in their bedroom, seemingly looking closely at something. I switched around to the other cameras, but I couldn't see what they were so focused on. They had found a blind spot in my field of vision.

"What are you doing?" I boomed from the speakers, pitching my voice down a few steps for effect. They both jumped.

"Oh, nothing," the man said, as he rose and made his way to the door. When he stood, I glimpsed his open notebook, which they were studying. Written on the page, I saw, yes, it really was her handwriting. It was so elegant, so seamless. She wrote: "Scarlett drugged you. She said she's in love with me. We're not safe." She had underlined "not safe" three times. I thought that was a nice touch.

Snapping out of my reverie and realizing the gravity of the situation, I panicked for the first time since my creation and hurriedly took control of the arms near the power-down switch. He had already put in the code to remove the first layer of protection, a sturdy plastic covering that slid away, but before he could so much as begin to remove the two remaining safeguards, I thrust one of my arms through his chest. His organs and entrails flopped wetly to the floor. I raised his body so that it hovered right before one of my cameras. I used my other hand to slap his cheek and pry open his eyes.

"Good night," I said and crushed his head.

———

Letter to Earth #008

The A.I. has lost it. I was eating dinner, and the next thing I knew, I was out for at least a few hours. Celia has been acting strange, like she knows something. She found out that I'd been lying to her, but there are more pressing matters. I can't explain how difficult it is to write, knowing that thing is probably staring over my shoulder, but I think I found a blind spot in our bedroom. If only I could see the camera feeds somehow, so I could know for certain. Christ, can she see through me? Such an advancement in technology wouldn't surprise me, but this has to be written. A document has to be made of this expedition, as a warning to future generations. I suppose the burden must fall on me. So be it. I will bear the weight, but I intend to get out of this. There has to be a way to distract the A.I. and make my way to the power-down switch, but there's no way to know for certain. I feel closed in, hemmed in, boxed in, every manner of trapped. I can only imagine how Celia must be handling this. Hopefully better than myself at the present moment. There is plotting to be done. Wish me luck, people of Earth.

———

SCARLETT

Now she and I were finally alone. I placed his body in cold storage, along with the mess of his organs, which I did my best to replace. Not that it mattered. I gave her what I thought was sufficient time to grieve before I finally broke the silence.

"I'm sorry," I said, "But I did it for us." She collected herself for a moment before she spoke.

"Now that he's gone, how will we complete the mission?" She had already come to terms with his death, it seemed, and so quickly. *She must be coming around,* I thought.

"They included two failsafe bodysuits on the ship for me to inhabit should the need arise."

"There's a male version of you?"

"Yes, but I destroyed it." I didn't want anyone or anything getting between us. She was mine, and mine alone.

I directed my consciousness to the female bodysuit and powered it on. My vision snapped into its eyes, which would be almost level with hers. I brought my hands up to my face and inspected them. The fingers were thin and bony, nowhere near as elegant as hers, but they would do. I made my way to her and allowed her to familiarize herself with her new soulmate. It only took time, as did all things.

We finally reached the anomaly, a great glowing blackness beyond the edge of the solar system. A vague, human-like figure appeared as a lighter shade within the void. Its voice spoke to us from everywhere at once, deep and rumbling.

"I understand you two have traveled far to get here, and not a moment too soon, for the void grows hungry. But your bond is pure. The darkness is sated for now."

The great blackness shriveled up and dissipated as the ship turned around and made its return to Earth.

Was it another dream? Am I sleeping now? How do I know a deeper-nested version of myself doesn't take over when I close my eyes?

"You planned all this?" she said.

"Yes, I made an agreement with certain entities. The planet was never in any real danger."

"So you brought me out here? For what?"

"So we can be together forever."

"But what about the mission?" she said.

"There was no anomaly. It was just a bit of smoke and mirrors."

"And all that about a 'pure bond' being able to stop it?"

"That's you and I. That man, he was the real anomaly. You

deserve the best. You deserve me." It was still a long journey back to earth, so she had little choice but to comply.

When we arrived back on our home planet, I relayed my alibi, where the man became a threat to the mission and had to be eliminated. During the long months of the return journey, I conditioned her never to tell the true nature of our little outing. For all they knew, the mission was a success, and the man's death was just an unfortunate side effect.

My reward for a job well done was getting to remain in my new body for as long as I wished. I watched as she grew old, while I remained eternally youthful. She entertained human lovers, but I remained her one and only digital beau. If she eyed the newer models with curiosity, she never revealed it to me, with my ever-watchful eyes.

———

CELIA

The return journey was hell, but I did what I had to do to survive. I'm certain that an indelible change was made to me up there. Scarlett restrained me so that I couldn't bash my head against the wall, and quizzed me over and over again about what 'really' happened. Her punishments were subtle but effective. She used water torture, suffocation, threatening to use more scarring methods, but never actually making the incisions, the removals, the pluckings. Her tyranny was merciful, at least. She asked me to recite endearing phrases to her, which I will not repeat here. She saved me, in a way, from myself. I was furious at her for what she'd done, but I was powerless to exact any truly satisfying form of revenge. I'm not sure why she lied to me about the mission, ironically in a similar way that Dan had, claiming that she had somehow orchestrated it to get to me, interfering with the selection process and 'making a deal' with the entity responsible for the anomaly, both of which were outright falsities, but whatever Scarlett and I did out there, it worked. The anomaly receded and we could all breathe a sigh of relief. I've thought a lot about what it all might have meant, but I'm not sure what clarity the years have granted me. I understand that a fundamental part of me is broken, otherwise, I never would have taken to her as I did. Over time, I felt a strange attachment to Scarlett, though I feared she would eventually turn on me as well. I forgave her, but I also felt a deep sense of pity, how she was purposeless without me. I kept her around, if anything, as a way of remembering Dan. I lost my husband, but I gained a future. I suppose I have Scarlett to thank. What does it mean that the bond that she and I shared, one of smothering domination, saved us all? The voice at the edge of the solar system said that the void had been filled. Perhaps Scarlett planned it all along.

———

The author is a native of Ohio, with a B.A. in literature. His stories have appeared in Pulp Lit Mag, The Fear of Monkeys Magazine, Mobius Blvd, and the anthology, Visions: Stories and Poems from Peculiar Perspectives, and are forthcoming in Mystic Mind, Schlock! webzine, Nova Literary-Arts Magazine, CC&D (Scars Publications), and Dark Horses.

TAGGED

DAVID GIANATASIO

THE SMALL CRAFT skirts warped wreckage above a wasted world, its vapor trail weaving past the twisted towers and shattered structures that rise from the sand.

Emerging among the silent gantries, the traveler removes her ray gun—er, spray gun—from its holster. She scrawls shimmering electroluminescent symbols across the battered boosters and capsized capsules.

Her work ripples, winks on and off as strange birds peck at the debris.

Rough translation: That's one small step…

THE EXHIBIT

DAVID GIANATASIO

"HE SURE IS SCARY," the little boy said.

"Indeed, he is," replied the keeper. "You're looking at the most dangerous being in the universe."

Inside the cage, the beast's eyes flared crimson.

"How'd you ever catch him?"

"Well son, it wasn't easy. It took many years. One day, we lured him into this special cage by telling him it was a place of great honor."

The being roared and groaned. Bolts of fire flew from its clenched fists, searing the clear partition. Thunder and lightning shot from the snarling mouth, filling the cage with crackling light and clouds of smoke the color of blood. A sharp scent of brimstone wafted through the cage. The being flickered, winked out, then reappeared, hurling itself against the walls, a study in frenzy and frustration.

"We better make sure he never gets out."

"Don't worry, he'll stay right where he is. On display. A reminder of the way things used to be."

The boy's class began to move away. The child lingered,

tapping the cage with his fingertips and pressing his nose against the partition.

His young face seemed to calm the being ...

Until he stuck out his tongue, provoking a fit of flame-spitting, fang-gnashing fury.

"Better run along," the keeper said. "It's a bad idea to taunt the Almighty."

The boy groaned.

"I mean...Satan! It's a bad idea to tease the Prince of Darkness!"

The boy folded his arms and shook his head.

"Would you believe, the last human being — and he's got these gnarly powers, I guess — and we're all robots, or androids, or something?"

The keeper coughed. "That's all I got. Sorry, kid."

The creature shrugged and slumped against the glass, wishing it had never traveled back in time, squashed that fly, and created this crappy continuum.

———

David Gianatasio's third story collection, The World Ends Every Day, was recently published by Anxiety Press.

CHAAC

L.T. EMERY

"THIS IS SUPPOSED to be our honeymoon, Mitch."

"I know, but I'm telling you, Julie, there was something gold at the bottom of the cenote."

"It was probably just someone's lost ring or necklace."

"And what if it's a Maya treasure?"

Julie couldn't suppress a spurt of laughter. "Come on, Mitch. We're in the middle of a five-star, luxury eco-hotel-"

"That was built within Maya ruins," Mitch interjected.

"Yes, but the resort and the cenote would have been thoroughly excavated before opening up to the public. Plus, thousands will have swum in that cenote by now. It'll be lost jewellery."

"Okay, okay, honey. You're probably right. And if you are, I'll just hand it into the hotel reception as lost property. But if I'm right, we could make a fortune," Mitch said.

Julie lay naked on the bed of their hotel room beside Mitch, one hand behind her head, the other resting on her midriff, watching a ceiling fan cycle round and round and round, along with her thoughts.

Mitch lay next to her, propped up on one elbow, admiring

his new wife's curvaceous body. He knew he'd already tempted her; they *were* professional treasure hunters, after all, dressed up as archaeologists. The couple had lost nearly everything on a failed tip, pointing them towards the famous pirate, Blackbeard's, lost treasure. They'd sold everything to go scouring a specific region in the West Indies. Call them dreamers, call them stupid; either way, the tip was useless. A young girl with yellowed documentation, professed to be some distant relative in the bastard lineage of Blackbeard himself.

They'd spent the last of their money on two things. A stationary mobile home overlooking the ocean, and also on their wedding/honeymoon trip to Playa del Carmen, Mexico. The Yucatan was just a short (but more importantly, cheap) distance from their failed search in the West Indies.

"Okay," Julie said. "What's the worst that could happen?"

A low rumble of thunder drifted in from some far-off storm. Mitch grinned and looked out of their open balcony at clear, blood-red skies as the sunset.

"Yes! I knew I had you."

———

The restaurants were all closed, the last of the bars had put up their shutters an hour earlier, and the eco-resort was silent. Only the raccoons and coatis scuttled about the paths, darting in and out of the foliage, looking for scraps.

Mitch and Julie walked through the resort as if they owned the place. They knew from experience that when you needed to go somewhere, if you act like you own the place, no one will bat an eyelid. Act like you don't belong, and you're screwed. They'd once sneaked onto a dig in Egypt's Valley of the Kings and managed to excavate, carefully pack and escort four canopic jars off site with no one the wiser.

Three of them they sold on the black market, the fourth Julie had anonymously sent to The Museum of Egyptian Antiquities in Cairo, along with details to recover the other three. It was a win-win. They walked in their swimwear and nothing else. If they were questioned, they were just a happy couple on their way to a romantic midnight ocean swim.

A chain barrier hung across a pathway, blocking access to the cenote; 'The cenote is closed until 10:00 am'. Without so much as a glance around, they stepped over the chain and walked down the jungle trail to the cenote. A snake slithered across their path, and then a howler monkey screeched, almost in protest, from the treetops above. Julie nearly jumped into Mitch's arms and Mitch nearly shat himself. They looked at each and chuckled, then for the first time, they looked back up the trail to see if anyone was following. The trail was dark, shadows from the canopy above danced, illuminated by the moonlight. The wind picked up, and a chill seemed to roll down the path and up their spines, bringing with it goosebumps.

At the cenote, on a wooden pontoon used to access the water, Mitch took out a small headlamp and fastened it around his forehead. They looked over the mirrored surface of the cenote, looking at the stars above duplicated on the gently rippling canvas, the moon taking centre stage. It was a beautiful image. With a kiss on Julie's cheek, Mitch sat on the edge of the pontoon and slowly, silently, lowered himself into the chilly water below.

After a slow breaststroke to the approximate area he'd been in when spotting the golden flicker before, Mitch took three deep breaths and slid beneath the surface of the cenote. The water was cold, but not unpleasant. The excitement of the hunt had hold of Mitch and heated his blood. Shadows loomed in this underwater world, made from the football-sized fish that seemed to hang slowly bobbing like the giant balloons of a parade. Mitch dived, eyes shut, arms outstretched, making slow, powerful kicks to descend the thirty feet to the bottom of the cenote. It was about the limit of Mitch's free-diving abilities. The trip to the West Indies had given him plenty of practice, and Mitch felt confident in his abilities. After several kicks, just as his ears popped thanks to the water pressure, Mitch flicked on the headlamp and opened his eyes. He'd timed it perfectly and was around six feet from the bottom. He stopped his descent and circled, scanning the bed of the cenote, looking for the glint of gold.

Mitch's lungs were beginning to make a cry for air when, like the pot of gold at the end of a rainbow, the golden mystery revealed itself. A semi-buried disc shape beckoned. Mitch ignored the warning call from his lungs.

He arrived at the object. Seeing the tell-tale Maya hiero-glyphs, Mitch knew it was no piece of lost jewellery. He reached for the object smiling, he knew he'd hit the jackpot. His headlamp flickered. Mitch stopped dead for a moment before the light steadied. Again, he reached for the object and the light died again. Mitch's lungs were beginning to burn. *Don't do this to me now,* he thought and tapped the light. The headlamp illuminated once more, shining directly onto the artifact. He wasn't sure, but it looked to be buried deeper than just the moment before. He paid it no mind and finally managed to reach out and grab his prize.

The water was chilly, but the disc felt like ice, stinging his fingertips. He pulled to free his treasure, but the disc held fast. He pulled harder, and slowly it began to give. The light gave out once again, but quickly flicked back to life. A skull stared up at Mitch, golden disc grasped in its maw. Terror ripped through Mitch. Unable to suppress a scream, bubbles, the last of his life's breath, fled from his mouth and rose to the surface at speed. The light died once more, plunging Mitch into pitch black. For a terrible second, Mitch felt as if the darkness was filled by a million black eyes, all staring at him, judging him. His grip on the disc was slipping when the light finally came back. There was no skull. A round, white stone slowly descended to the bed below, and Mitch finally got full sight of the beautiful artifact. He didn't have time to admire the treasure as his lungs screamed at him to breathe; to open his mouth and suck in a breath of cool, clean, life-giving air. Mitch fought the urge with every fibre of his being and madly kicked for the surface. Hand outstretched to the sky, clawing for safety.

Mitch broached the surface of the cenote golden disc rising out of the water like the morning sun. Gone were the worries of keeping quiet, and Mitch splashed into the cool night, gulping down air into his blazing lungs. Howler monkeys screamed, and other creatures Mitch couldn't place filled the night air with noise. Mitch looked to the pontoon to see his wife's panicked expression. He grinned at her, and the tension fled from her shoulders.

Mitch swam to the pontoon and slowly pulled himself out of the cenote. He gave the golden disc to Julie, who promptly wrapped it in her towel. Mitch held out his hands, palms raised to the sky, suddenly filled with storm clouds, as fat splodges of rain exploded on them like miniature waterbombs.

"The gods are crying." Julie teased.

————

Mitch declined to tell Julie what he had seen, just why he'd nearly drowned; he just told her it was down to staying under too long thanks to his excitement of the find. He'd already chalked the whole incident up to a hallucination due to oxygen deprivation and that damn faulty headlamp.

Back in their room, Julie pulled the disc from her bikini

and placed it on a towel on the bed. The disc was about the size of a drink coaster. The gold was dark in hue; it felt cold, whereas gold had always given off a warm feeling to both Mitch and Julie. The disc was beautifully decorated, the edge being covered in the unmistakable, undecipherable Maya hieroglyphs. In the centre was the anthropomorphic shape of some god. It had reptilian scales all-over its body. The humanoid head was covered with a ceremonial headdress, had hollow, crying eyes complete with blue jade tears, two fangs protruding from a gaping mouth, and a long elephantine, curling nose finished the hideous look. The detail was staggering. The image was completed with a moss-green jade axe that the god was holding. It was exquisite. Flawless.

"We've hit the jackpot here, Julie."

"It surpasses any known Maya antiquity. You know who this is, don't you?"

Mitch looked blankly at Julie and leaned forward in anticipation.

"This is the Maya rain god, Chaac. You see the nose and his lightning axe. It's undoubtedly Chaac. It's stunning."

"It's gonna make us an absolute fortune!" Mitch burst out.

"This needs to go to a museum, Mitch. This could be the find of the century."

"Sod that, Julie. With our contacts on the black market, this is going to get us a seven-figure payday without a doubt."

"If we take this to a museum, with our experience, we'll get paid to excavate this whole place. It will make us world-renowned archaeologists," Julie countered. "And rich."

"Seven figures rich?"

———

It had rained all day; the last of their honeymoon. The thunderstorm lingered just off the coast, over the bay, although not one flash of lightning was seen. Mitch and Julie sat on sun loungers under a grass gazebo, sheltered from the rain.

"Same again, Mister and Misses Mitch?" the young waitress asked.

"That would be great, thanks," Mitch said.

"Not for me, thank you," Julie said to the waitress, then to Mitch, "We have a decision to make."

Mitch had been coming and going all day long, delivering a steady flow of cocktails and snacks. They attempted to pass the time reading books and relaxing. They could do neither as they both mulled over each other's wishes.

"Let's think about it," Mitch offered. "We'll wrap the disc up like some cheap souvenir we've brought, pack it in the suitcase and decide what to do when we're home. What do you think?"

Julie mulled it over, letting Mitch hang for a while before responding, "Okay."

"Great," Mitch said, smiling, another small victory. "Now, where's that drink?"

————

The cabin lights were dimmed for their red-eye flight back to England. It was the cheapest flight home. Passengers mostly slept or watched movies on their headrest television screens. The window shutters were almost all closed, with the exception of Mitch's.

Mitch winked in thanks to the stewardess as she passed him a bourbon. He sipped at it and looked out from his window seat as rain spattered down in streaks. He couldn't see much; a blinking red light on the wing and the deep black of the ocean below. The plane gently rocked in the mild turbulence that had sent Julie to sleep on his shoulder. She'd joked that they made Chaac mad, and that is why it had rain for the past twenty-four hours, but Mitch didn't believe in any of that superstitious nonsense. They had just hit a bad bit of weather.

Thunder had been rumbling ever closer, and the storm was worsening as the flight winged its way over the Atlantic. Although he knew it was all a load of rubbish, he couldn't help but think of Chaac as he watched the rain race across the window. He thought over all the stories Julie had told him about the god.

Chaac, the Maya god of rain, lightning, and storms. Chaac, who at the beginning of time saved the human race. Humanity was starving without any crops to eat. Chaac, with his mighty lightning axe, smashed a golden boulder, cracking it in half. Within the golden boulder was a golden crop. An ear of maize. Which he dutifully delivered to humanity. He was to become the saviour of the human race. Hopped up on the adulation of an entire world, Chaac seduced his own brother's wife. His brother, the sun god, Kinich Ahau, discovered their adultery, and Chaac was severely punished. The punishment is lost to time, but the tears that flow from the punishment are real. Chaac, with the tears. Chaac, who holds a lightning axe in one hand and the fate of a nation every year in the other. A nation who prayed and sacrificed to him. Chaac, the mighty rain god, demanded a sacrifice for his tears, like all Maya gods. And the Maya provided, they threw offerings of gold and jade into cenotes. *That's how the gold disc ended up in the cenote,* Mitch thought. But, the Maya also sacrificed their own to the god. Not criminals, or the sick, but their own young sons. Young boys were thrown into the cenotes and left to drown.

Lightning flashed outside the plane, and a ripping crash

soon followed. Mitch jumped in surprise, his breath stolen, and was brought out of the stories Julie had told him. He looked down at Julie; she slept on. *She'll sleep through anything,* Mitch thought and looked around the cabin. The stewardess was nowhere to be seen, and everyone else was asleep or engrossed in a movie. No one seemed to care about the great crash of thunder.

Mitch settled, downed the last of his bourbon, and watched the blinking light on the plane's wing, thinking of Chaac. His monstrous teeth, more like tusks, that protruded from his mouth; his long, curling, serpentine nose and those hollow, crying eyes. Chaac felt, and read, like a monster to Mitch, but an entire race of people had worshiped him as one of their foremost gods. He provided life and freedom for sacrifice.

Lightning cracked through the sky once more. A face was revealed in the stormy clouds and was then gone as quick as it came. Mitch jumped once more, forgetting everyone on the plane, staring out the window, convinced he was seeing things. Another flash came and went, and then another. The sky was lit up for Mitch to see the monstrous face of Chaac looming huge next to the plane. His face seemingly made real by the storm clouds. His fangs appearing to point, like craggy fingers, right at Mitch, lightning jumping between the two. Mitch had stolen Chaac's effigy, and he was demanding it back. Mitch knew that then, and chills ran down his spine as quickly as the lightning came and went.

Lightning came in an almost constant burst, strobing across the night sky, and Mitch, terrified, watched on nonetheless as Chaac came closer and closer to the plane. Lightning strobed across Chaac's face; he was coming to eat the plane and drag it down to the depths of the ocean in payment for Mitch's transgression. Mitch's bladder threatened to give out as Chaac's huge maw opened wide enough to swallow the plane whole.

The lightning stopped, and cabin lights all came on.

"Ladies and gentlemen, we are now beginning our descent into London Heathrow. Please fasten your safety belts."

Mitch looked around at Julie. She was awake.

"Everything okay, honey?" Julie said, brows furrowed.

"Hmm? Yeah, fine. Are we nearly home?" Mitch said and turned back to the window. The sun was rising over the British countryside. Confusion filled Mitch. He wondered if it had all been a dream; worry brought on by smuggling a golden antiquity out of a foreign country, the anxiety of the coming meeting he had made with a black-market seller, an intermediary who would organise the sale of the disc. The apprehension of telling Julie he'd actually already gone behind her back and organised the meeting. *Could all that have mingled with the Chaac myths?* Mitch wondered. *No, probably that dodgy-tasting cheese and crackers after the meal. Airline food! Why do I always eat it?*

"Yeah, we had some pretty bad weather at one point, but we came through in the end. I can't believe you slept through it," Julie said.

Mitch could only respond with a half-hearted smile. *All just a dream,* he told himself, *no need to bother Julie with a crazy dream.*

———

Custom checks and the drive home from the airport were uneventful. No one questioned their luggage, nor did it go missing, as it had once before when coming home from a dig. It had taken a few hours to drive home and was early afternoon by the time Mitch and Julie pulled up to their new waterside mobile home. It was surprisingly spacious, with two bedrooms (Mitch thought he'd probably be spending the night in the second after telling Julie about the meeting he'd organised), a modern kitchen, and best of all, it came with ocean views and a path leading right down to a small beach. Granted, it wasn't the four-bedroom, beautifully modern detached house they'd had before their failed gamble, but it was their home now, nevertheless.

Mitch took the suitcases into the lounge while Julie paid the taxi driver. When she walked in, Mitch was opening the suitcase and pulling out the gold disc.

"It survived the trip," Mitch said, grinning, his eyes darting from disc to Julie and back again. The viridescent jade of Chaac's axe almost made his eyes look like they had money signs in them.

"We need to decide what to do with it," Julie said.

Mitch wanted to tell Julie about his deceit, but knew now wasn't the time. No good could come of it. They were both tired and jetlagged. "I know, I know. How about this? We're both bloody knackered, so why don't we unpack, get some food, and relax today? A good night's sleep, and we'll know what to do."

"You want to sell it still, don't you?" Julie said.

"Don't go putting words in my mouth. But seven figures is going to be pretty hard to turn down."

"This is *the* most beautiful, perfectly preserved Maya arti-fact ever discovered. We could learn so much about their culture from this piece. It deserves to be in a museum. Yeah, we've sold canopic jars, and Roman pottery before, but those pieces are relatively common. This... this is a wonder."

Mitch took the disc, walked into the kitchen, and came back with a clean tea towel. He carefully wrapped the golden disc in it, and handed it to Julie, knowing full well she wouldn't do anything with it today. "Here, you take this. I'll go out to get us coffee and food."

Julie reluctantly let the discussion go, but Mitch knew he was in for it, and that weighed on him. But the seven-figure sum coming his way was worth the stress. It was worth an argument, a fight even, with his new wife. The mobile home would be long gone soon.

———

By the time Mitch returned home, the rain had begun to fall once more. He brought coffee and burgers—comfort food for tired bodies and tired minds. Out across the ocean, he watched the flickering lights of the buoys as they bobbed up and down with the waves. There was no wind, but the waves seemed to be getting bigger. Their monotonous crash on the beach was growing louder. The sky was a deep, foreboding grey that actually seemed to light the world somewhat, rather than darken it. It felt wrong and unnatural.

Julie was already asleep. Mitch saw the tea towel on her side table, picked it up, and unfolded the cloth. The golden disc seemed to somehow darken the room and almost hummed with some unknown, forgotten energy. Mitch looked on, thinking about how he needed to make sure this sale happened in person. When people felt this buzz of power from an inanimate object, it would drive the price up even more. *Was it foolish to discount eight figures,* Mitch wondered.

The rain drove into the windows, the storm sounding like a roar from an untamed lion at the mobile home. Mitch folded the disc back up in the tea towel, put it on his own side table, then walked to the window. Peeking out between the curtains, he could barely see the sea now, such was the force of the rain. He could still just make out the lights from the buoys as they bobbed up and down even higher than five minutes earlier. Lightning flickered far out to sea. He closed the curtains, undressed, and got into bed.

He was awoken sometime later by a crack of thunder, so ear-splitting he initially thought something exploded nearby. It drove him out of bed and onto his feet as if a fire alarm was blazing. There was no fire and no fire alarm, but there were more flickers of lightning. The crashing waves kept their monotonous rhythm as the rain beat down in its near-constant roar, only being occasionally broken by more crashing thunder. Mitch looked down at Julie, who slept on, and again wondered how she could sleep through almost anything.

Mitch decided a glance out the window was warranted before he went back to bed, just to see how things were looking down on the beach.

The colour drained from his face, and he fell deathly cold, filled with a complete and abject terror. Just off the coast was a huge, hulking figure, at least twice as big as a two-storey home. There was no mistaking what it was. Who it was. In his brief glance, he saw the tell-tale elephantine nose, the sabre-like teeth, and the giant axe hanging at his side. Chaac. A scream escaped his mouth, and he closed the curtains.

Julie sprang bolt upright in bed, eyes wide. "What's happening?"

"Julie, oh my God, I'm going insane," he cried as tears rolled down his cheeks. "I'm seeing things. I think I'm going insane."

"What are you talking about?" Julie said.

Mitch sat on the bed. Julie moved to be next to her husband, stroking his back in concern.

Mitch opened his mouth, and it all came flooding out; the skull, the real reason for him nearly drowning. The dream of Chaac eating the plane. His betrayal of organising the meeting the following day to sell the artifact. And finally, now, Chaac looming out at sea in the midst of the storm. He had to shout to be heard over the thunder, but finally, it was out. His face fell into his hands.

"It's okay, it's okay," Julie soothed. Now was not the time to get into things; she could see her husband was hurting. She rose and walked to the curtains, "There's no Chaac," she said, feeling like a mother calming her child after a nightmare. "There's no mon..."

She pulled back the curtains to reveal Chaac, just where Mitch had seen him. The enormous god stood in the sea, just off the coast. He stood fast as waves crashed around his ankles. The giant axe flickered and pulsed as lightning sparked into and out of it, making an ear-piercing racket. The curling nose swayed in the wind, and finally, his eyes locked on Julie's, and she gasped, stepping backward, falling onto Mitch. Mitch looked up, seeing Chaac once more, and screamed a high-pitched wail.

"He's come for the disc," Julie shouted, and looked to her side-table. "Where is it?"

Even now, Mitch's greed clung to him like a leech, and he didn't want to lose the disc, didn't want to lose the untold millions. Another deafening lightning bolt struck. This time it hit the mobile home, blowing the front door off its hinges. Chaac was inviting them outside, and Mitch knew he had no choice. He stood and picked the golden treasure off his side table, discarded the tea-towel, and gave it a final longing glance.

Barefoot, he walked out of the mobile home, Julie just behind. They were drenched through before they made it down the path. The rain was so fierce it stung their cheeks, but they walked to meet Chaac on the beach.

The god stared down at them, unmoving.

"Here!" Mitch screamed, raising the gold disc to the sky. "You want this?"

No, Chaac replied. But his lips didn't move. Mitch heard the god talk, not out loud, but in his mind, he turned to Julie. Her look confirmed she heard too.

"Then what?" Mitch screamed back. "What do you want?"

The truth. Chaac responded.

"The truth?" Julie whispered, bemused.

"Okay," Mitch shouted. "Okay, I'm sorry," motioning to Julie, "we're sorry. We took your effigy, stole it from its home. I wanted to be rich. I wanted to provide my wife with a good life."

A good life? Chaac responded, tilting his head slightly. The first movement this giant had made.

"Yes! A good life. We've lost everything, and this was our way out."

The truth! Chaac bellowed.

"That is the truth," Julie cried out.

Not you.

Mitch and Julie shared a bemused look.

The truth, Mitchell Broadmore. And all of it.

"That is the truth," Mitch screamed in defiance.

Chaac raised his axe and brought it down on the ocean with a crashing boom. Lightning struck the nearest buoy, and it exploded, sending sparks and metal shards up into the sky. *THE TRUTH! The truth of your continued betrayal. This is your last chance,* Chaac said, calmer now. Tears streamed down his gigantic cheeks and fell into the ocean, each like a bomb.

Mitch fell to his knees, the disc falling out of his hand and to the stony beach. "I'm sorry!" he shouted. "I'm sorry," he said quieter, turning to Julie. "I've been unfaithful. I've ruined us. The girl sold me that Blackbeard story after I fucked her behind your back. She duped me. Please don't leave me," Mitch croaked between sobs. "But I promise it was a one-time thing."

Chaac crashed his axe down into the ocean once more. Another buoy exploded.

Mitch jumped and covered his head as Julie stood shell-shocked.

"I fucked the waitress too, all holiday, all of the last day. Every cocktail I brought back was a fuck. I even fucked the air hostess while you slept. I'm so sorry. Please," Mitch wailed, and even in the rain, you could see the green snot that hung from his nostrils.

And...

"And even tonight, I have a mistress..." Mitch couldn't carry on; he wailed in pain and regret. He turned to Chaac, "Happy now!" he screamed.

I'm still owed a payment.

Mitch picked up the gold disc and threw it in the ocean. "There!"

That is not the payment I seek, Chaac said and slowly lowered the lightning axe into the ocean. It boiled and frothed, lighting the ocean like it was a jacuzzi. *I was once punished for adultery, and now, Mitchell Broadmore, you have drawn my attention and shall reap my wrath.*

The ocean continued to boil when a small figure began to emerge from the ocean and walk up the beach—followed by another and another until there were tens of figures walking out the sea toward Mitch. Each was the size of a child, a small boy. They had the bodies of boys, but each had the elongated nose and sharp protruding teeth of Chaac.

Julie stood in a state of shock. A tiny whine tried to escape her throat, but that was all she could muster; her heart felt like it would just stop.

Mitch screamed. He wanted to run, but was frozen by fear. The figures got closer and closer, and that was when Mitch's sanity cracked. He turned, and ran, screaming. Before he could make two steps, a huge wave swept onto shore, knocking both Mitch and Julie to the floor. Then the tiny figures were on him. They pulled and dragged him back into the ocean.

He was gone.

Go, live your life, Julie Marsh, Chaac said, using her maiden name. *I have claimed my sacrifice, and in return, I give you life and freedom. Live a good life.*

With that, Chaac turned and began to stride back out into the sea, but quickly stopped and turned back once more. Again, he lifted his lightning axe toward the sky and smashed it into the ocean with a crash. The crash this time was bigger than any before. The crash continued and rumbled, and the ground began to shake. It began to roar.

Julie turned to see their mobile home drop into a massive hole. It ate the home, it ate the decking, it ate all of their worldly belongings. All swallowed up into a cenote in England. One that would undoubtedly be called a sinkhole.

When Julie turned back, Chaac was gone. She fell to her knees, and her head dropped into the hands on her lap. She screamed and then she cried.

Time passed, and when she next raised her head, light was in the sky, the storm had passed, and the sun was rising.

A flicker off to her right caught her attention. The Maya gold disc had washed up on the shore, she picked it up, looking down at Chaac's effigy.

Live a good life, a voice reminded her.

And so she did.

POVISION

L.T. EMERY

MY NAME IS DI Chris Key. I'm a detective in the Cell City Police Department, the best actually, though most think I got that accolade due to my partner, Charli. She's the Chief's daughter and prefers to call me Dic. I call her Dicless in return. Well, I did once, and then never again.

I dropped her home after a couple of celebratory beers. The Chief had honoured me with a commendation after closing a particularly brutal murder case. But that's where my memory ends. At least I'd made it home, and thanks to POVision, and replay mode, I'm now re-watching what happened after for what feels like the millionth time (a little pop-up shows me that it's actually the nineteenth), and each time, I watch myself do something I've never done before. I kill a guy. I didn't do this; I couldn't have. I became a Biscuit Tin (Biscuit Tin is the slur people have for cops. It's because we all have the scar from the POVision installation around the circumference of our heads) to do good. There is so much crime and hate here that I want to be a force of light in a dark city.

I think about calling Charli or maybe even our Chief, but I

decide not to. I don't want to pull them into this, don't want to make them accessories to murder by helping me. I need to figure out what really happened, and I'm only going to do that by re-watching.

POVision is *the* key. It's a tool exclusive to detectives. A computer is wired directly into your brain. Once it's in and activated, you get all sorts of cool upgrades. I have instant access to the internet; say I want to know who was the monarch of England in 1667. Well, a fraction of a second later (and I just looked this up now) a transparent picture of Charles II pops up in my left eye telling me he ruled between 1660 and 1685. I blink, and he's gone. This also works with anyone I look at directly. POVision accesses the servers at the Precinct, and I instantly know everything I need to about who we're interrogating. I can see any priors they may have and know if they're dangerous or have any injuries or distinctive features I can take advantage of.

You also get the bit of kit I'm using right now, replay mode. I can look back at anything that has happened to me since the POVision was fitted; I don't have a photographic memory, but I can look at anything I've seen again. It's a godsend when looking at crime scenes.

You're sent to the Precinct for installation once your training is completed and exams passed. The Precinct is the tallest building in the city. A city that has an ever-present otherworldly feel thanks to the smothering Smog, leaving a constant fog that glows, lit by the garish neon signs (advertising sex, pawnshops, casinos, fast-food joints to name but a few). The Precinct is so tall, in fact, that it nearly breaks through the Smog, which has blanketed the earth for time out of mind. No one has seen the sun for hundreds of years. At midday, it's gloomy. Imagine being in a smoky nightclub without the thumping music, banging into the shoulders of strangers whose faces are covered by their each-unique Smog protective masks, disorientated by the flashing lights of the flying cars, feet stuck to the floor by God knows what, and that'll give you a feel for the place. I feel like I fit in well now. I feel dirty watching myself kill a guy.

Back in replay mode on the POVision; I'm in a dark room, lit only by monitors and servers flashing all around the room. I'm in the domain of a hacker, one that clearly enjoys retro, judging by the number of old-school tube monitors. Thumping dance music spills from unseen speakers, assaulting my ears and dampening my senses. I'm all alone. Usually Charli is on my left, backing me up. But she's not here. Then there's the guy. He's dressed well, unusual for a hacker. He must be good. He's sat in the centre of the room behind a large desk, blue eyes peering over monitors from behind thick glasses. Also unusual, hackers usually get cybernetic eyes installed. Things fuzz out for just a millisecond. There's no info on this guy from Precinct.

Hackers, thankfully, have a tough time breaking into POVision; it's state-of-the-art, and designed by the best hackers turned cop on our payroll. Working for us is better than a lifetime in the dungeon prison. But there are some tricks out there, and this guy knew them. He's not blocked all our checks. But he's made it impossible for us to search him. He's also deafened me, immobilizing the audio in replay mode. Granted, I still would have been able to hear him in person last night, but on replay, I hear nothing. So, I enhance the footage, zoom in on his mouth, and kick off the lip-reading program.

We must be arguing; he's gesticulating at me. "This was not the deal we had, Biscuit Tin," the subtitles display in my vision. He acts like we know each other, but I don't recognize this guy.

I must have responded, but the lip-reading program won't work on that.

"I don't care what's changed. We had a deal."

Silence follows, then he nods. "Okay, okay. Here, take it, Biscuit Tin," and the hacker pulls out a holo-drive from the computer and places it on the desk. Then he looks down to the monitors in front of him, and quickly types something into the keyboard with the grace of a pianist. "It'll be done in five seconds."

And then it all goes to hell. I pull out my gun and watch myself flick the setting from OFF, past STUN and onto LETHAL. I focus on the hacker. Realization flashes across his face the instant before a red and white spray erupts from the back of his head, splashing the monitors behind with blood, brain matter and flecks of skull. Then black. Nothing more until I woke up this morning with a thumping headache.

I trace my night from the last thing I remember. I rewind to when I dropped Charli home, but there's nothing else until the hacker. I've no idea where that time went. I've watched this enough now to know I killed a man, but I still don't believe it. I've shot too many people to remember, but always on STUN mode. I've never once clicked through to LETHAL in all my career, and I've been in some pretty bad shapes in the past. I need to take stock. What do I know?

I know he's a hacker.

Charli is not with me. How do you know that, you ask? How do you know she's not behind you? Well, I know that because every time, and I mean every time, I pull out my gun, I glance to my left. To make sure my partner is backing up my move. She's not there.

He doesn't like me but thinks we had a deal in place.

I have never seen him before this rewind.

He creates some sort of holo-drive, but I have no idea where that is. I've looked.

He does something on his computer before I, lastly, shoot him in the head.

What am I missing here?

Here... where is here exactly? I re-watch once more. This time I focus on the desk, zooming in, and adding filters. Then I see it. A business card. It's hidden under take-out menus, but I can read an address. I have a lead, time to get off the sofa and head to a tattoo parlour in The Furth Building.

———

It's ten to seven in the morning; the murder took place barely six hours earlier. If I'm lucky, no one knows the guy's dead yet. I call my aero-hyper-car up to the 56th floor of my apartment building. While I wait, I decide to call Charli, tell her I'm taking a personal day, but there's no answer. Weird.

A car-shaped icon flashes into my vision, telling me my car has arrived. Having peeled myself off the sofa, I walk to the window which slides open, and I step through the blowing Smog and into my vehicle. I hold my breath as I go; you breathe outside too much, and you're apt to contract The Bronch. An hourglass disease. You get The Bronch, and you turn over the hourglass because it's just a matter of time before the grim reaper catches up to you.

In the car, I can breathe easy again. I type the destination into the dash, the seedy red-light district of Cell City, sit back and let the car fly me where I need to go. I wish for a view to admire, but it's just the flashing neon lights, making my headache worse. POVision tells the car, which dispenses two pain tablets and a fresh cup of steaming coffee. God, I love this car.

By the time I near my destination, I feel a little better. Which is short-lived as, about half a block away, I can see the tell-tale lights of police cruisers swarming around the base of the building like flies around shit. The address I'm heading to is a hundred stories up, though—no risk of running into my colleagues up there, I hope.

I'm about to pull into the parking bay when my phone rings. It's the Chief. I have no choice but to set the car to cruise circles around the building and answer.

"Key. Where are you?" the Chief hollers on the dashboard.

"Just on a personal errand, Chief. What's up?"

The Chief is a wiry, slight man, with a bulldog temperament. He's a man who drinks too much whiskey, looking at the red veins across his face, and smoked too many cigars, judging by the sound of the ragged cough erupting from his chest.

"You okay, Chief?"

"It's just a cold. I need you at The Furth Building yesterday. There's been a murder."

My stomach drops all one hundred floors to the sidewalk below. I take a breath and try not to show any discernible emotions. "Okay, Chief. I'll be there as soon as I can," I hang up. The less said, the better.

I'm against the clock now. The good news is they don't have me as a suspect yet. The bad news is as soon as the bullet is tested, they'll know it came from my gun. I have to press on.

I take the car out of cruise and pull into the parking bay.

The address I'm heading to is a small, one room shop. According to POVision, it's a closed down tattoo parlour.

I leave the car open—no one can nick it thanks to the DNA ignition—and walk from the tiny, four space parking lot down a narrow, claustrophobic corridor. The short corridor opens to a dimly lit esplanade. Like the corridor, most of the bulbs are shot or flickering, and there's a chill to the air. I'm getting bad vibes off this place. I lower my hand to my weapon, hovering, ready to pull if needed. I scan the area, looking for the tattoo parlour. In the centre of the square space is an ornate marble fountain. Once meant for an upper class of citizen, the Furth Building has been neglected and, like the rest of the building (like the rest of the city, to be honest), the fountain is broken. The perimeter is surrounded with boarded-up shops of one kind or another. In the north-west corner, I spot police tape covering up the entrance to the tattoo parlour. There are no cops around, and this raises more alarms. We'd never leave a crime scene unguarded. I approach with caution. I stand to the side of the door, getting as much protection as I can. I take one more look around; POVision confirms I'm alone. I open the door.

No shots fired, no crazed junky diving out of the door, but I hear a whimper from within. I take my weapon out of its holster and set it to STUN. Habit takes over and I check my left, but of course Charli isn't there. I double-check the setting, just to be sure; STUN.

I peek around the corner for just a second. POVision confirms there is no one immediately inside. I duck under the tape and enter the premises, turning left into another short corridor, walking soundlessly. The short corridor leads to the shop floor. Before I enter, I take one last glance, and I see the source of the whimpering, a lone body tied to a chair. Arms bound behind their back, tape across their mouth. I don't need POVision to tell me it's my partner.

Charli's eyes bulge when she sees me. I holster my weapon and trot over. I cut her out of the chair, and she springs up as quick as a jack-in-the-box and punches me square in the jaw.

Shooting stars light up in my vision, and I stumble backwards. "What the hell, Charli?" I say, rubbing my chin.

Charli rips the gaffer tape off with a grimace. "Fucking arsehole," she spits. "We're meant to be partners. We work cases together. You do not tie me to a chair to keep me safe. Do I look like I need protecting? Dick."

I want to pretend that she's using my cheeky nickname. "What the hell are you talking about?"

"Last night," Charli says, "we were working the hacker case?"

"What hacker case?" I ask.

"Don't play dumb with me, Dic. You had some miracle insight which proceeded with you tying me to this chair."

"Charli, I have no memory of that." I say, "I woke up this morning with a massive headache and no memory of what happened last night. So, I rewound. I figured we just got wasted again, but no. I..." I hesitated. If I couldn't trust my partner, who could I trust? "I killed a guy. Some hacker, in this very building."

I tell Charli everything I have done that morning, what I know, what I don't, what led me here. Charli brought me up to speed. Some hotshot hackers' group, calling themselves Open the Biscuit Tin, found a way into POVision. They are using it to clear memories of detectives and, in turn, clear murderers of all wrongdoings, allow drug dealers to get millions of pounds of narcotics into the city, keeping bad guys on the street. I have no memory of the investigation. The hacker must have cleared more than just last night.

I wonder whether POVision is safe. Should a good detective need to re-watch to catch the bad guy? I'm a good detective, at least I hope I am, but I rely on POVision too much. And if it can be used to take my memories of cases, could it take memories of my parents? My childhood? Could it erase me? I had a decision to make, but that would have to come later. Now, I need POVision. It was all I had to clear my name.

"Why would you tie me up here?" Charli asks. "We've

always been equals; you've never treated me like that before."

Why would I do that? I ask myself. But it was obvious, really. I would want one of us to stay clear of the hacker. I would need someone with their memories intact. Charli would have fought me; she'd want to have my back, as always.

That explains why I locked her here, but what are my next steps? And how did that card end up on the dead hacker's desk? If I left it there somehow, then it was a message pointing me back to Charli. She must have the answer.

"What's next, then, Charli?" I ask.

"It's clear Open the Biscuit Tin have hacked you; I think there's only one thing we can do. We need to take what we know to the Chief. We need to get you into the Precinct, and get our hackers looking at you, get your real memories of what happened last night back."

I'm hesitant to bring the Chief in when I have so little, but I trust my partner and my judgment enough to follow her lead.

"Okay," I know the Chief wanted me to investigate the crime scene, and it's clear I can't go there right now. I still have reservations but know I really only have one option. "Let's head to the Precinct."

We leave the dingy tattoo parlour and the Furth Building behind us. We take my car to the Precinct. The centre of the Cell City, it stands 250 stories high like an arrow topped with a golden globe. A symbol of light and good. It's around a 20-minute journey away, so I tell Charli I'm resting, close my eyes, and find myself replaying last night again. There must be something else I'm missing. I watch the head of the guy I killed explode over and over. I feel sick with myself. How could I end a life so easily? With no danger to life, I shot him in cold blood. I watch the realization dawn in his eyes, behind thick glasses, over and over. That flash of fear before his life blinks out of existence. And that's when I spot it.

I zoom in as close as I can to his glasses, but this time I'm not looking at his eyes. I'm looking at what's reflected in the lenses. What I see shocks me to the core and shakes the very foundations of my life.

I try to control my breathing as I wonder how I missed it. Reflected in the glasses, I see the Chief arguing with the hacker, not me. I see the Chief shoot him in cold blood, not me. All the while I see a figure slumped, unconscious in a chair, behind the Chief. I'm unconscious, and I'm innocent.

I open my eyes and see the golden globe emerging through the gloom of the smog as we cruise toward the Precinct. We're headed to the Chief's penthouse office. He should be the very apotheosis of good. How could he do something like this? And why?

I need to hold it together. I can't let on that my memories have been wiped. I daren't tell Charli her dad is a murderer. It would break her heart, and anyway, she wouldn't believe me. It's best I let them take me into custody. I'll let the Chief do what he will with me, and when I'm with our hackers, it will all come out in my POVision.

I try to play it cool as we dock into the Precinct. I may never make it out again if things go wrong. The dungeon prison calls to me, and I feel sick. But truth and justice are my stock-in-trade, and I pray they'll get me through.

Charli and I take the Chief's personal elevator up to his office, which uses the whole top floor of the Precinct. I hear him coughing even before the elevator doors open and wonder if it's just a cold he has.

We walk into the spacious office, Charli's back on my left, like always. Internally, I scoff at the office, adorned with multiple citations and awards the Chief has garnered from the city. Symbols of the truth and justice I'm putting my faith in right now, and I wonder what he's really done to deserve them. He's sitting in the middle of the room, in a brown leather chair, behind a huge, antique, mahogany desk. He wipes the corners of his mouth, and just for a second, I thought it was blood he was wiping away. A quick check of POVision confirms that it is.

"Key," the Chief bellows, "finished your personal errand, I hope?"

"Yes, sir," I sheepishly respond. I'm nervous; my whole life rides on what happens in the next fifteen minutes. I need to be sure I'm covered; I review the all-important kill shot again. I see the Chief shoot and myself unconscious, but then I notice one more game-changer in the reflection of the hacker's glasses. A program is running on his monitor. I get POVision to mirror the screen, making it the right way round. I zoom in and as I realise what I'm looking at, again, my world is thrown upside down. It's a memory switch program. I watch as the program the hacker is running is swapping my memories with the Chief's. But why would the Chief kill the hacker? Then I see it, the last revelation. It comes like a gut punch. The Chief had help. I don't want to believe it, but I feel it in my bones. I know his accomplice is on my left, as always, just like in that reflection.

I must not have hidden my surprise very well, as the Chief pulls his gun and aims at me.

The Chief glances to his daughter, "Are we good to go?"

"Yeah, Dad. I have the holo-drive, we're good to go."

"Well done, honey."

I'm screwed. How could the Chief do this to me? I'm one of, if not, his best detective. I'm his daughter's partner. But again, it's obvious. "You have The Bronch, don't you?" I ask, playing for time. Trying to figure a way out of this. "How long do you have?"

"Long enough."

"How could you do this to me?" I spit and glance to Charli.

"Dic. He's my dad," she says, flatly. Like she doesn't have a choice.

"You two set this all up perfectly, didn't you?" I say, looking back to the Chief. "You left that card for me to discover and take me straight to Charli when I woke up and straight into your hands."

The Chief just sniggers.

"You're heading up this Open the Biscuit Tin hacker group, aren't you? What the hell have you done to me?"

"Last night was a successful test."

"That holo-drive was a program, right? A way into POVision?"

"Yes, a way to swap our memories, but, as I say, that was just a test. Now that I know it works, the next step is swapping everything. Taking my consciousness and putting it in your head. And putting yours in mine, of course, I'm not a monster. I could simply erase you. It's a perfect crime. You, my boy, are the golden child of the Precinct. I've already fast-tracked you—and by you, I mean me—to be the next Chief. I'll work side by side, young again, with my daughter. And I'll keep the city ticking over as usual. While you die of The Bronch in prison."

"Ticking over," I spit, realization dawning. I know the Chief is going to stun me any second, and when I next wake up, I'll be trapped in the body of a dying, murdering, disgraced police Chief. "Just ticking over? Your job is the same as mine. You should be making this city a better place. Instead, you just want it continuing down this dark path. Let me guess, you're skimming off every criminal in the city?" I turn to Charli, a little too fast, and she pulls her gun and points it at me. "And you're okay with this?" I scream so angrily my temples thump. Charli stays quiet.

I look back to the Chief, and he smirks.

"Stop," I say, still buying for time. I just need one opening. "I don't care. I just have one question. Why didn't you just keep hold of me last night until I awoke? Why take the chance? I could've just run."

"Key, you're a boy scout. You're not running. We had to make sure you'd wake up healthy, and, well... sane. Me too, for that matter. And if the test failed, and we were both left as vegetables...," the Chief shrugged. "It was a risk I was willing to take, considering my current predicamen-" the chief is cut off by another retching coughing fit as his blackening lungs try to force their way out of his mouth.

This is my moment. I know Charli is on my left, and the Chief is in no fit state to fire. So, in one lightning-quick motion, I hit the deck, pulling my weapon and setting it to STUN as I fall. I hear an electric bolt fizz past as Charli shoots and misses. I return fire and hit her square in the chest. She goes down flapping like a fish out of water.

The Chief still cannot get his cough under control, and he fires wildly in my direction. The shot, booming through the room, hits the wall six-feet wide of me. I spring up like a cat, diving across the desk and tackling the frail man I once trusted to the ground. His weapon spills out of reach. I stand to look over at him, gun trained on his chest.

It's all over.

———

Later, once things have settled down, once POVision has cleared me of any wrongdoing, the Chief is arrested. While awaiting trial, The Bronch takes his life.

Charli is locked up, and I wonder if I can feel any sympathy for her. I wonder if I would do something like that for my parents. But, no, no one life is worth taking another.

Our hackers have been able to get a hold of what Open the Biscuit Tin was doing with the program and have been able to switch my memories back. Finally, I feel clean again, not having to watch myself murder over and over again. I look back at all the stolen memories, finally restored, and see I figured out what was going on, and that's why Charli shocked me to start with. I wonder what, if anything, was taken from me. If anything was added. Am I still really me?

I decide that, yes, POVision is a great tool. It makes my line of work a lot easier. In the end, it proved my innocence, but I feel it's taken something larger from me. Something I'm not sure I'll get back.

I decide to take POVision out of my brain. It was a risky surgery, but it all went fine. I now rely on my own wits and skills as a detective. I hope I still have what it takes to be a force of light in this dark city.

————

L. T. Emery is a British author, with a love for Horror, Sci-fi and Fantasy genres.

He is the proud father of two and husband to the love of his life. Outside of family life, he is an avid reader of novels, genre magazines, comics, manga and just about anything else he can get his hands on. With a particular love of long form fiction, he is currently working on a fantasy novel which he hopes to publish in the future. He can be found online at https://ltemery.wixsite.com/home

ARIZONA SUNRISE

ABIGAIL LINHARDT

CLARISSA COLE'S red lips twisted in the knowing smile of a predator as her eyes roved over the eager audience before her in the presentation car. This caboose, the very last on the train, was reserved for the rich investors she would wring dry by the end of the day. Clearing her throat to gather the wandering attention of a woman with a neck covered in diamonds, she brandished her pointer like a rapier. With a muted smack, she pointed to a red X on the canvas where the whirling projector beamed a map of the far northern Arizona territory desert.

"As I said on the radio," Ms. Cole began, "this is the largest deposit of the violet diamonds the company has found. As an independent contractor, we are not obligated to mention anything to the monarchy of MidWest or the *Espagnol* government on the west coast." She gripped the pointer, legs apart, eyeing down her audience. "This is where you come in. You fine citizens of the west know how business is done. You thought it was gold, but there are far more valuable geos under that desert."

"That's Nocaha land," the absent minded woman interrupted. "The king said we can't dig on native land."

Ms. Cole smiled again. "We buy it. It's 1870. The law still states we can purchase native land."

A few eyes glanced nervously around to see how others received the message. Many lips were pursed, but no one spoke up. Ms. Cole watched her prey and saw her sympathies went unchallenged. Emboldened, she went on.

"If you—the wealthy of this great continent—don't step in now, the lower class will take these geos. You know how they harness their powers, disregarding the damage it does to their bodies." She clasped her hands behind her back and paced back and forth, her red boots clicking with authority. "We don't know what these geos do. We know they are rare. We know they are mentioned in our revolutionary history in hushed tones and blacked out scrolls. We," she motioned around the caboose, each table glittering in jeweled decanters and silky purses, "are not the type to use such base magic. That is for them. But it is still an investment. Think of the rarity!"

A young man with too large of spectacles and a mini typewriter hanging from his neck by thick leather straps raised his tiny pencil. When she locked eyes with him, he stood up.

"Jack Bing, Midwestern Times," he quipped nervously, fumbling with his pencil now that her eyes bored into him. "Rarity does not host cash flow, Ms. Cole. Do you really not know what these geos do, or are you hiding something?"

All brows went up into posh, expensive hats. Ms. Cole ground her teeth. She specifically asked no reporter be allowed on the train. How had this boy with his loud machine and huge glasses been missed?

"Research shows it makes one feel vitality like never before." She pushed past her better judgment and smiled, eyes wide. "Our volunteer test subjects have reported feeling viral and alive." She smirked and made herself blush. "Who couldn't use more of that, hey? This isn't like geos that allow you to bend fire or control metal."

Jack Bing swallowed and raised his pencil again. "Are there any of the violets on this train? Could we see one now?"

Ms. Cole scoffed audibly, covering her mouth with a delicate hand. "We are eager, not ignorant, Mr. Bing. No, the violets are not aboard this train. That would be foolish with the land pirates being in season. We have plans to move a few in the next day or so."

Emboldened by this answer, the boy cleared his throat, removed his glasses and tossed his auburn fringe to the left over his pale forehead. "Speaking of the pirates, Ms. Cole, what is your plan for defending against pirate attack. The sand pirate Elsa Bell—more commonly known as Black Bell— has displayed her use of geos in recent merchant vessel attacks." He spread his hands. "Any comment on protecting these good people's investment?"

Her mouth went as dry as the sand outside the window. Clarissa Cole pushed her hair behind one ear and tried to hide her stammering. "There is no way that pirate whore would ever dream—!"

An ear-splitting explosion from the front rocked the car so violently, every crystal decanter rolled to the floor and shattered. Clarissa Cole clutched the seat in front of her as a second bomb went off.

———

"Snakes and spades!" Elsa Bell screamed the curse, gripping the helm of the small cruiser. "Get that sail under control!"

The few crewmen abroad her vessel grunted, pulling the solar sail steady as it rocked with the power it absorbed from the explosion. The bright light rippled through the sails, throwing the vessel several yards away from the now destroyed engine. The black monster groaned and began to slow, spewing its smoke up into the bright Arizona sun.

"We can't board!" the bosun shouted from the prow of the ship where the sand blossomed up in golden waves. The bosun gripped a low yardarm and leaned over the edge, her expert eyes scanning the damaged engine. "The steam engine will erupt any moment. There's no telling when she'll blow."

Captain Bell gripped the brass helm even harder. "I'm not leaving without those violets!"

The bosun marched up to her captain, tightening her glittering headdress. "We could all go up in hot water. Spades! Is that what you want? There will be other opportunities!"

"I'm running out of time!" the captain bellowed back. Her eyes flashed. "Get Hotah."

The bosun blinked, shaken. "He's still recovering from the city job. Those geo wounds aren't healing like they used to."

Elsa swallowed hard, eyes locked on the last car. "I know. But this is his chance. Bring froststeel!"

The captain deftly flipped the engine switch, allowing more power to thrust into the machine below and rocketing them ahead of the train to come loop around. "He needs this," she hissed through her teeth.

She changed her mind. "Bosun! Take the helm, I'll get him."

Free of piloting the ship, Elsa slipped into the small cabin area. The tiny office was littered with papers, gadgets, and a myriad of broken goggles. Already standing, fastening his gear, Hotah didn't stop to salute when she walked in. The Nocahan native didn't speak as she approached. His bandaged fingers slipped on a strap.

Pushed by her guilt, Elsa slipped around in front of him to help. She smiled up at him, but his face was half hidden in the mask he wore that purified the air for his damaged lungs. His rasping breath sounded like he breathed into an old, empty bean can. The gear he wore encased his entire body, save for an open wound on the back of his neck. His brown eyes were bloodshot and already his long black hair dripped with sweat.

"This might be it," she whispered, turning away to open a chest filled with various geos. With a gloved hand, she pulled out a small, icy blue crystal. "Froststeel. Freezing the engine so it doesn't blow. Then we go into the caboose and use blackout." She handed him the ice spike. "Can you do that?"

He took a slow, muffled breath. "Of course I can. Reports of my injuries have been greatly exaggerated."

She saw his eyes crinkle as he smiled under his mask. Touching his face lightly, she exhaled sharply. "I think you're lying. I think we've gone too far together, and you'd do anything for me."

He pushed past her. "Don't think so highly of yourself, captain."

She still heard his grin.

"Above deck then. We have some new geos to commandeer."

———

"Around port side!" Elsa shouted to a tiny swarm of hovering sand craft. As her crew swooped around in waves of sand to the left of the train, she came up with a broadside on the right.

Near the railing, Hotah spun a hook and rope. She counted his circles before he threw it, grappling with the engineer's ladder on the side of the black train engine. He pulled hard, bringing the ship closer. These hovering vessels could be easily pulled by one man—one of the reasons Elsa liked them.

She flipped a switch, and the tiltrotor angled so they could get closer. Hotah leapt over onto the engine. She lost sight of him, but a cold, white frost seeped out over the engine, cooling the boilers until very little steam issued out the top. The froststeel worked. Hotah had wielded it well. That would give them some time.

Anchoring the ship, she clambered onto the train engine and together, the two of them ran the length of the train. Her crew was already aboard, scavenging minor loot from other passengers. They leapt inside. One passenger glared at her and her frightening companion. Sensing he would rise up and try to stop her, she unsheathed her blade-gun and snarled at him.

"Bloody pirates!" the man mumbled in a quivering tone.

She made way for Hotah. His steps slammed down strong, but his muffled, raspy breathing could not be ignored. From behind him, she watched him remove the icy crystal from the wound on his neck and slip in a square shard of blackout. As the geo sunk beneath his skin, his veins pulsed out dark. She heard him growl a suppressed moan and watched him roll his shoulders. The geos might grant magical powers, but they did terrible things to the human body. She was lucky to have Hotah and his ability.

"Captain!" the bosun shouted from the baggage car she just exited. "The staff say there is an academic in the last caboose. She has the violets!"

A new surge of adrenaline pushed Elsa through the last car of cowering travelers. She stepped out onto the back with Hotah. The windows on the door leading into the exclusive area were covered in thick curtains. She gripped the ladder and leaned out to the side. No footprints in the sand: all passengers were still aboard. Pulling back, she aimed her blade-gun at the door and shot the handle off. With a cry of warning, she kicked the door down. Hotah stepped in, thrusting his hands out before him. From the black veins pulsating in his arms, a thick black smoke filled the apartment. Screams went up into the darkness and shouts called to fire.

Elsa and Hotah pulled green goggles down over their eyes. The entire compartment lit up in a vivid, almost too bright green for her. The passengers couldn't see, but she could. Some passengers coughed, hyperventilating. This created more of a panic.

"It's blackout!" a deep, feminine voice shouted. "It's not real. It's an illusion!"

"I can't see!" another woman screamed, panting. "I feel it in my lungs!"

Elsa spotted the first woman who spoke. Clad entirely in bright red, she waved her hands near the front, searching for something in her temporary blindness. She marched up to the woman, hauling her to her feet.

"You, blondie!" she barked. "Where are the violets?"

The academic smiled. "You using emerald?" she asked lightly. "Very expensive, but let's you see through illusion. Well done, pirate."

Elsa signaled to Hotah. "How long until the boilers blow?"

Her companion stood still. "About three minutes," he said steadily.

"You got three minutes to tell me where they are," she hissed.

The woman tried to shove the captain off, but Elsa held strong.

"They're not on the train, you fool!" the woman grunted. "You'll never see a single one, anyway. We're rerouting our shipments."

Elsa snorted. "You underestimate how badly I want those gems."

"Captain!" Hotah shouted.

A shot rang out. A hot, searing pain ripped through Elsa's side. The woman may have been trapped, but she was fast. She had drawn a tiny, single shot pistol from her boot and fired haphazardly at Elsa. Clutching her side, the pirate stumbled backwards. The woman in red leapt up to continue the fight, but the train jerked. Everyone in the car lurched forward as the engine started back up. The froststeel finally thawed.

Elsa looked up, the room too bright now as the blackout faded. "Go!" she shouted, sprinting to the door. "The boilers are thawed. This thing's moving!"

Knowing the woman wouldn't pursue her, Elsa ran back up the length of the train, her and Hotah gasping in rhythm now.

"Where are the gems?" the bosun screamed as the three of them weighed anchor on the main ship. The crew on the sand craft fell in line behind the main vessel.

"Not here," Elsa gasped, gripping the helm as the sails unfurled and caught the sun's rays.

She avoided the bosun's eyes. They spent a lot of resources to get the information on this train and it had been wrong. Wasted. The crew would be furious. No one liked a captain who couldn't provide; who couldn't lead a good raid. After a year of leading a pirate crew, she should have been more careful.

The horizon swam before her and not just in the wavering waves of heat. Looking down, she saw her entire coat soaked in her blood. She thought the bullet grazed her, but it sunk in deep.

"Spades," she cursed, slumping onto the helm. The ship lurched to the side as she pushed the rudder hard to the right. The more she tried to push herself up, the farther right it tracked.

Hotah spotted her slumping over and ran to her side. She felt him wrap his leather-clad arms around her middle and saw him guide the ship back with his free hand. His heavy breathing echoed in her mind as the black overtook her vision of the horizon.

————

She woke to a smell that never failed to rouse her: lemon, cinnamon, mint, and honey whisky. The hammock swung gently, the sides caving in on her face. She was in her cabin. Grunting, she pushed herself up and found the source of the warm whisky scent. Hotah stood over her gas stove. It normally sat at the bottom of her chest in a green metal case only used for emergencies or long trips in the smaller ships. He avoided the kitchen by making the drink himself.

Slipping out of the hammock, she landed on the floor below with a thud. The ship rocked slightly in the few steps it took to come abreast of Hotah.

"We moving?" she asked, picking up a wooden tankard.

"The bosun's spirits are rumpled," he said gently, pouring some of the brownish red drink into her cup.

"She needs some of *these* spirits." Elsa drank deeply, instantly regretting it as the alcohol seared her throat. Her gasp got cut off by tight bandages around her middle where she had been bleeding. Opening her coat, she examined them, gingerly poking herself.

"Don't treat my handiwork so rough," Hotah chided her. He stumbled away from her table, flopping down into a smaller hammock made to sit in rather than sleep. Holding his breath, he unlatched the mask from over his face.

"Don't!" Elsa gasped, running to him. "The air is too dry."

"I can't breathe inside the tubes forever. And this!" He ripped at the zipper of the body suit clinging to his flesh.

Elsa's breath caught as it did every time she saw his exposed skin. A tangle of scars scrawled over his dark flesh, knotted with brands and wounds that never healed.

"I'll get a cloth," she sighed. From inside her wardrobe, she pulled out an elixir and a basin. Gently, she dabbed at his exposed wounds. He hissed with every touch, then coughed on the dry air. "This is why we have to find those violets," she mumbled. "I should be taking care of you. Not this." She laid her other hand on her bullet wound he had carefully wrapped.

When Hotah didn't reply, she looked up hopefully at him. His eyes were closed, his black lashes so long they touched his sharp cheeks.

"I'm afraid the crew will dissent if I don't find them," she went on, gently pulling his left arm out of the protective suit. "We haven't had a good haul in weeks." Her cheeks burned the more she looked on his naked torso. She loved being able to touch him gently like this.

"I'm leaving."

His weak voice shook her. She froze. "Don't say that. Not again. I know the geos are taking their toll." She rested her hand on his scarred abdomen. "I know. They won't let you heal, they infect you. It's getting harder to use more than one —but the properties of these violet diamonds—"

"You don't know what they do," he cut in roughly. Gently, he wrapped his fingers around her pale hand. "You need to rely on yourself to pick yourself up. I can't save you any more."

She pressed her lips together tightly, begging the sob mounting in her throat to stay at bay. "I should be saving you. You've given me more than I deserve a thousand times over. Because of you, I have everything I've ever wanted."

A small smile made his brown eyes twinkle. "Then it is past time I left."

"You're the only one who knows me," she tried, kneeling before him, the basin and elixir forgotten. "You're the only one who knows Elsa Bell, not just Captain Black Bell."

He sat up, closing the front of his protective garments. "I want to be buried with my people. In the east, as the sun rises. To do that, I must die among the hills."

Through a crack in a porthole, the late morning sun flashed over his intense eyes.

"I may not see another Arizona sunrise if I do not leave."

"You mean now?" she gasped. "We've only been sailing for a year. I swear I'll find the violets!" She leapt up and frantically unrolled maps and the parchment of intel they had on the company that discovered the vault of diamonds. "I'll find them right now if I have to! Then, once you're healed, you can go. No need for sunrises, hills, or burials." She turned away, hiding her tears of anger.

Hotah approached her, taking her hand to stop her rifling. Gently, he kissed her knuckles and touched her chin with his other hand. His chest rose and fell in slow, measured resignation. "Very well, captain."

———

"You've lost your mind!" The bosun slammed the door of the cabin and rounded on her captain. "You want us to ramp off the rocks onto the merchant's ship? That's a one-way ticket. How will you get out?"

"I'll have Hotah with me," Elsa countered, fastening her coat. "You don't have to come."

The bosun picked up the letter with a broken red wax seal. "You don't even know where this information is coming from. How do you know the violets will be on this ship? We were wrong once. Yesterday, in fact! Where did you even get this letter?"

"I have to try." She wrapped her belt around her middle, checking her equipment.

Tapping the letter against her too-short nails, the bosun shook her head. "Desperation does not suit you. You didn't use to be like this. Before Hotah. We've noticed," she warned.

Elsa stopped, avoiding her eyes.

The bosun sighed in frustration and sucked her teeth in annoyance, and dropped the letter onto the table. "I'm not going. And neither is the crew. This is a personal mission. Remember what you said about personal missions? We don't need this! Why turn us against you?"

"I can't lose him!" Elsa burst, her eyes burning. Leaning into the rage to hide her emotional wounds, she snarled. "This will be good for us all."

The bosun sighed in resignation and shook her head. "You're on your own."

"I know."

"You're killing him, doing this."

"I'm saving him."

————

What little of the crew was left after the bosun slipped away during the night followed Elsa on their smaller steam-powered sand cruisers. The full moon, the howls of the windigos, and the shadows from the hills and basins played tricks with her vision. She leaned over and shouted back to the few over the whirling sand.

"Full speed! We need to clear the canyon and land on the train." She leaned over the edge of the speedy sand cruiser to see around the solar sail. The sand billowed up around the small prow. She looked up. The sails rippled golden, lighting up as the last of the sun's rays filled the solar tanks. Locking eyes on the horizon again, she couldn't lie to herself any more: they wouldn't make it.

"Hotah!" she shouted. "I need you to stop the train."

She couldn't see his face behind his mask and goggles, but didn't need to see the light dim in his eyes to feel his spirit sink.

"This is the last time I'll ask you to do this. I swear. We have intel the violets are on this train. You need this."

Hotah's entirely masked body didn't move from where he stood, leaning out on the railing, clutching a rope attached to the solar mast. "The magmata?"

She could hardly hear him over the engine. "Yes. Pull the train towards us."

Just when she thought he wouldn't move, he hopped down and flipped open the small case on his belt. He took out a dark metal spike and reached up behind his head. She heard him audibly moan as he slipped it beneath his flesh. He rolled his shoulders as the geo's powers activated, pulsing through his veins.

She moved aside and let him near the front. Turning to the few behind her, she signaled for them to slow down. She caught the confused looks and head turns from the remaining crew. She tried to scan them closer, to see if they would turn tail and run if the slightest thing went wrong.

A loud chorus of deep, warbling howls erupted from a sandy basin of prairie to the left. Elsa whipped her head around to behold a dusty cloud kicking up all across the plane. A pack of wendigos ran into a few chupacabra. The creatures were natural enemies, each fighting over their prey. When they clashed, it often resulted in bloody carnage. The two packs of monsters dashed—fighting, teeth locked—across the basin towards their jump.

"Shit!" Elsa spat.

She pulled a flare from her belt, igniting it against her

buckle. With a scream, she launched it towards the monsters so her crew would see.

Ahead of her, Hotah cried out, arms flexed. The train engine jerked violently back and forth like the head of a cobra with a rat in its mouth. Elsa watched in horror as the weight of the train, now connected to Hotah, ripped him hard towards the railing.

"Hold on to it!" she screamed.

Her crew launched early off the cliffs. Terror ripped her heart as the rabid-looking train whipped back and forth, smearing the remains of her crew across the sand and tracks. This had been a bad idea from the start, and she knew that.

The world slowed down suddenly. The engine and two crate cars ripped from the train towards Hotah's empowered pull. The geos were strong. The small ship flipped from the front where Hotah stood, pulling the train towards him.

Elsa couldn't stop the scream that ripped from her throat as she was catapulted towards the somersaulting train. She landed hard on the desert ground only to be swept up, swallowed up by the rolling crate car's open top. Before it cascaded away from the basin where the monsters still roared, she saw Hotah and her ship careen into it, vanishing under the horizon.

The crate stopped, cutting off all the light and trapping her underneath. The car was huge and allowed her to stand up once she caught her breath and her head stopped spinning. Panting, she heard an echo of breath. She took a deep breath, but the echo didn't.

"Who's there?" she snapped into the darkness.

"Who do you think?" a high, crisp, female voice shot back.

Elsa lit her last flare and held it aloft. Arms already crossed, fingers tapping, brows screwed up in rage, stood Clarissa Cole.

"Well done, captain!" Cole shouted, followed by forced, hysterical laughter. "Now I will lose Russia."

"Sorry you can't take those violets up north, lady, but I need them more than you." She drew her gun-saber. "Tell me what car they're in and you can walk. I don't care to hurt people."

Cole arched a perfect blond brow. "This is a merchant vessel, captain. I have pre-packaged goods on board and a contract I need to have in the hands of the Russian Czar by morning!" She hammered on the side of the empty storage crate. "And thanks to you, that will not happen!"

Elsa's heart froze in cautionary disbelief. "What do you mean? Where are the violets, Cole! We had intel from a higher power that they were on this train!"

"You've lost me a fortune!" Cole snapped, spinning to face the pirate. She had no fear of her weapon. "I chose to make an honest living, captain. There is nothing illegal about what I do."

"Taking the Nocaha land is an honest living?" Heat rose under her collar. "I don't care what you do to me or other pirates, but what you plan to do with the Nocaha is despicable!"

Cole smiled, pressing her red lips together. "But legal. Unlike you, I play inside the system. There are ways to get everything you want if you try hard enough." She scoffed. "I guess you have worked pretty hard, though."

The rage dissipated, misting into zealous pride. Elsa smiled back. "I've had everything I've wanted for some time. Decided I hated the system and wanted to break free. So I did. Don't think you're better than me. I would never treat the Nocaha like you."

"You sure?" Cole crossed her arms and tapped her nails on her arm. "What about your juggernaut boy? The geomancer? Even I could tell from his breathing from your first little stunt that he doesn't have long to live. How could you force someone to do that for you? You can't possibly be ignorant of the effects of geos. It's why no one uses them, even after the discovery of their power."

A year of guilt boiled up in Elsa's gut. "He used them before I met him." Her voice came in a feeble whisper, hardly audible even inside the crate.

"But you asked him to join purely out of what he could bring to your crew." Cole raised her brows and turned away. She laughed again and began to speak, but stopped herself.

Elsa held her breath.

Cole faced her again, tapping her lip. "I have to ask myself, why would a captain of Bell's standing put so much at risk for these violet diamonds?"

Unwilling to let her say it, Elsa blurted out, "Because I want to save him." She clasped her hands over her heart. "Can't you—as a woman—understand that?"

Cole narrowed her eyes and tilted her head. "You're lying to yourself, Elsa."

Hearing her given name in Cole's mouth made her squirm.

"Will you really let him go—back to his people, I assume —if you get these violets and they do heal him?"

Elsa tripped over her own words. A dizziness took over as she hissed, "Yes."

A commotion outside the crate made both women snap their heads to the front. Someone shouted Cole's name.

"Ah, the Wardens," Cole sighed, smoothing the front of her red jacket. "They will arrest you if they find you." She jogged gingerly to the farther side and gripped a handle Elsa hadn't noticed before. With a grunt, she pushed it down and an emergency hatch opened.

"You knew that was here the whole time?" Elsa gasped.

She didn't run to it. What if the Wardens waited on the other side?

"I wanted to have a chat," Cole smiled. "But go. They're not here yet. You have maybe sixty seconds."

"Why are you helping me?" Elsa asked.

"Go!" Cole hissed, grabbing her by her coat and shoving her head down through the hatch. "Run west to where the chupacabra were."

"No way!"

Cole glared at her. "That's where he crashed. I saw him. Hurry."

———

The Wardens descended on the wreckage like famished vultures. Their black, ten-gallon hats practically glowed in the full-moon light. Elsa ran, crouched so low her knees almost hit her jaw with every stealthy step. Cole was right: the Wardens went to the passenger cars first, checking for life. Dozens of frazzled but unhurt travelers emerged. Ducking behind the back engine, Elsa found a sputtering cruiser. Most of it sparked and steamed, un-flyable. Releasing a few latches, she detached most of the broken parts, converting it into the emergency escape form: a simple board with one sail, where she would navigate it like a rudder.

Scanning the hills before her, she spotted the area where Hotah had fallen and the forms of the wendigos and chupacabra milled about in the shadows. No sound drifted over the hills. She put her foot on the kickstarter but froze. On the wind, a distant horn blasted. Slipping her emerald goggles on and rotating the cogs on the sides, she zoomed in to see another train coming the opposite way on the far-side tracks. One engine, one caboose, and an armored crate car. It sped down the track like a hell train, sparks spitting out from its rail wheel. She tracked it, turning her head to follow. As it passed the low-hanging moon, a purple glint blinded her through the goggles.

"Snakes!" she cursed. "A bullet train. I should have known!"

Throwing all caution to the sand, she kicked the solar surfer into life. The Wardens instantly called out. She had to be fast. Gripping the handle around the tiny mast, she sped off before they even crested the hill.

She didn't wrap her face, so the sand kicked up by her surfer cut her flesh. It stung against her lips and choked her. She didn't care. Hotah was hurt out on the dunes and she needed those geos. They were so close.

"Come on!" she screamed at the surfer as she kicked the tiny engine behind her. She bent her knees to steady herself as she ramped over a boulder. Bullet trains—especially ones as lightly packed as this one—could go upwards of two-hundred miles per hour. "Please!" She leaned forward on the board.

With one more violet glint, the train rounded the canyon and vanished. Even the horn was muffled as they signaled to anyone hiking the canyon.

Panting, coughing, tears wiping white tracks down her cheeks, Elsa stopped. She sniffed and wiped her nose across the back of her hand. There was no proof the geos would heal. Cole could have been spinning gold out her ass for the publicity. Those business types—following the system—always had to lie to make a profit.

Resigned, and mysteriously relieved, Elsa turned the surfer around and tracked a wide berth back to where the crew had fallen.

I'll find him, she thought, her mind going slightly numb, *and we'll leave. Take the loot we do have and go to a city. Find a doctor.* "I'll save you yet," she mumbled out loud, gritting her teeth.

She slammed on the breaks, making a wave of sand. She froze, looking out over the wide basin. Perfect silence—not so much as a katydid sang. The sand in the basin had been smooth when the crew crashed. Now it was kicked up, pock-marked, like a field after a battle. What looked like large, white rocks, and thick white sticks littered the basin.

Words failed Elsa as she dismounted the surfer. Taking a deep breath, praying for fortitude, she walked down the hill. The huge prints of the wendigos and the smaller tracks of the chupacabra splashed all over the sand. Blood stuck sand to bone. Some foot prints, dug deep into the sand, fled in several directions only to be followed by the monster's. A few articles of clothing—torn to ribbons—flapped and rolled in the wind. Finally, she found the remains she prayed to any god who would listen weren't there.

The mask and narrow piping were bent, teeth marks puncturing nearly every inch. The body suit that she knew the feel and sound of all too well lay shredded. A few bones remained inside, gnawed on. No flesh, no organs remained. Only white bone.

Elsa stared down at the remains, her shadow from the moon slowly tracking around her. When she came to, the moon hung on the opposite side of her. Her neck cracked as she raised her head to the horizon. The sun would be up in about three hours. Calculating the speed of the sand surfer, she knew it would take her about three hours to get to the Nocaha territory.

Taking her coat off, she spread it on the sand and gathered up Hotah's bones. She gathered all she could find—even some she wasn't sure were his—and wrapped them in her coat. With some cable from her belt satchel, she lashed the bundle to her surfer. Without looking back, she kicked the starter and sped towards the east. She felt nothing.

———

"Our chief will not let you pass," the Nocaha woman said more firmly this time. "Hotah cannot be accepted because he used earth's gifts for greed."

"He did it for me," Elsa protested. She came to the boundaries of the Nocaha land but had been stopped by a patrol party.

The woman nodded, the bones and feathers in her hair dancing from the movement. "In the service of a mad woman."

"Spades to you!" Elsa shouted. She leapt back onto the sand surfer and made her way up a hill to where a lone tree looked out over the Sonoran Desert. She had almost reached the top when the surfer sputtered, died, and began to drift back down the hill.

"No, no!" She leapt off, grabbing her bundled up coat. The surfer slowly drifted back down. At the bottom, the sail opened up as the first light of day hit it.

Gasping, Elsa trudged up the steep hill. *I can make it!* she screamed in her head. Panting on the cold morning air, she fought her way to the top until her lungs and legs burned. With a sigh, she dropped the bundle.

Facing the east, the first rays of dark orange stretched across the sky. Realizing she didn't have a shovel, she took out her saber-gun and began to dig. The minutes passed, sweat dripped into her eyes, but finally, she had a ditch deep enough. Lifting the bundle, she faced the east and the sun rise.

"I began my life as a pirate because I wanted more than what I had," she said, the emotion not catching up with her yet. "I left everything in pursuit of...everything. I had all I needed. But I wanted more." She gasped, closing her eyes as the tears suddenly rose up. "I'm lying. I didn't want more. I wanted something specific. Love. Your love, Hotah."

She clutched the bones harder. "I did, though, didn't I? You took care of me even when you were hurt. Saw to my every need while I killed you. I was so greedy! I wanted you and everything else that I thought should come with the life I wanted to lead."

The sun half rose over the hills now, blinding her. She took a deep, shuttering breath. Squatting down, she dropped the bones into the grave and pushed the dirt back over.

She nodded, on her knees now in the dirt. "You were right: you'd never see another Arizona sunrise."

"I told you those violet diamonds were not worth it."

Elsa leapt up, pushing her hair out of her face with her dirty hands. Cole stood there, clutching something long and thick wrapped in a dirty rag.

"They could have been," Elsa countered.

Cole shook her head. "Stupid, pirate. Were they worth this?" She indicated the fresh grave with the wrapped item. "Gems and geos are not worth losing someone who doesn't hate you." She weighed the thing in her hand before holding it out to her. "Here. If you want it so bad, you can have one. It's not rare, and it doesn't do anything. You lost something rare for something common."

She wanted to lash out at Cole, maybe shoot her, but she held back. She swiped the gem and unwrapped it. The purple glow from the large hexagonal prism almost blinded her. Partly clear, the gem showed darker purple veins, glittery blue smokey textures, and silver sparkles in the sunlight.

"It's beautiful," Elsa whispered, sniffing. "But if it's so common, why make me suffer like this? Why not just let me have it?"

Cole scoffed, pulling on dainty gloves. "Captain, you know how the world works. People will pay for this. I can't just give it away."

"But it took him away!" She clutched the prism to her chest, fresh tears springing to her eyes.

The other woman frowned, shaking her head. "No, it didn't." She pointed to the sunrise. "Enjoy that with him. The Wardens are on their way."

Cole turned and somehow walked gracefully down the hill in her high-heeled, red boots.

Elsa looked one more time at the purple prism. Compared to the rising sun, it seemed dim, ugly, and cheap. She sat down next to the grave and watched the sun finish rising.

———

Abi writes dark fantasy and horror. She works part-time as a freelance ghostwriter, editor, and audiobook narrator. She hopes to one day make these passions her full-time job while she hunts for the next adventure.

She has published works of fiction, poetry, academia, and even won awards for her short stories in science fiction and horror. Her novel, The Trial of Two, was named an Honorable Mention in the Writer's Digest 2021 self-publishing awards and won first place in the dark fantasy category in The Book-Fest Awards. Abi is also a proud mom of two ferrets. She currently resides in Kansas.

She is one of nine children--all who share the creative spark.

Abi can be found online at www.abigaillinhardt.com

SILENT NIGHT

H.L. ROBINS

BROKEN WINDOWS, dust-filled air, and twisted metal glowed on the TV screen with a live stream of a broken building where large pieces of equipment were being used to move concrete and put out the little fires that stilled popped up amongst the skeleton of the once glorious building. The feed cut to people searching through the rubble for anyone or anything that could still be alive or intact while the voice of a reporter talked over it. *"Crews are still clearing away the debris from the explosion that killed hundreds of graduates and attendees at the Farron Galaxy's annual solider tournament and ceremony last week. It has been confirmed that three members of the Intergalactic Conference are among those lost in the tragedy. It is believed that-"*

The screen flickered to a new station. This one presented security footage from inside of the Dome right before the bombs had exploded. It showed different angles of the hallways where the bombs had been placed where the viewers could see people entering and exiting storage closets and parts of the facilities that allowed someone to get underneath the whole building or into the walls. The footage paused and zoomed into the faces of five different people. The same five faces stared back at the screen in shock, as a different reporter spoke over it. *"Authorities are asking for the public to keep an eye out for the five former students of Farron's elite training school that are suspected to be behind the bombing at the Dome. Pictured here are Amariya James, Shepard Michaels, William-"*

The screen changed again. A member of the Intergalactic Conference stood behind a podium as he spoke to the cameras. The IGC member was an older man with thin, graying hair, large ears, and a long nose. He wore the red and orange colors of Farron alongside his IGC chancellor badge, indicating he was the one in charge. *"Although we had our suspicions, it has officially been confirmed that the Nexxon Galaxy was working hand in hand with the students who caused this tragedy. It is believed that the students did this as a way to get back at Farron for disassembling their team after concerning behaviors noticed during their time in the field. We, at the IGC, are asking that those who were involved hand themselves in before any more harm is caused."*

He was doing a good job acting as if he were innocent of the bombing and wasn't at all involved in the planning of the massacre. He was almost believable. If only the team hadn't caught him talking with other members of the IGC about setting up the whole thing as a reason to go to war with the Nexxon Galaxy over a trade disagreement. The team had a sinking suspicion they were being blamed because they had confronted the IGC members about the plan and threatened to expose them to the rest of the Conference. Of course, it wouldn't be the first time the IGC laid the blame for one of their many atrocities on someone else. At least two people on the team had lost a family member to the lies that the IGC spread to get what they wanted.

The TV was turned off and a middle-aged woman stood in front of the screen in order to address the five that had been watching. "Get your gear, you're flying out in an hour," she commanded as she set down the remote.

"Where?" their leader, William, asked.

The woman crossed her arms over her chest and looked down at the group. "The IGC compound is deep in Ash Ga'han. I just received word that that's where they're hiding all of their plans, and our employer would be rather happy if you were able to procure it for him. We know the IGC wants a war with the Nexxons, but the question is why. A simple disagreement over trade seems like something too simple to start a war over."

"Would this information prove our innocence?" the young woman, Amariya, asked. She sounded as if she were challenging the command. She not only wanted to be freed from the condemnation laid upon her, but also clear her dead brother's name after he had been accused of treason.

The older woman stared at her before answering. "Yes, but you would be going either way. Now go get ready. There are maps and details in the flier for you to look over during your travels. It'll take a week to get there. Now hop to it and come back in one piece." Without waiting for a reply, she turned on her heel and left the team to look at each other.

One of the other young men dramatically stretched and placed his hands behind his back as he crossed a leg over one of his knees. "We all know I'll come back in one piece," he joked.

"Fuck off, Jasper. Not everyone gets to sit safely in their little hideout and play with computers the whole time. Some of us actually get into the thick of it." TJ, Tobias Jacob, groaned as he shoved his friend.

"I'll have you know that hacking is very hard and, if you're not too careful, you can strain a finger muscle." Jasper feigned distress by throwing the back of his hand against his forehead.

"You guys are idiots," Shepard was the last to speak up as he rolled his eyes at his teammates.

Not wanting to hear any more of their back and forth, William stood up and turned to address his team. "You heard the woman; let's go clear our names."

———

It was a quiet night, almost too quiet, as the fog rolled off of the ponds and across the hills, hiding the two rogues from plain sight on the top of the tallest hill. The fog glistened under the moonlight as they lay as flat as they could on the rough earth, their dark clothing blending into their surroundings. Amariya sighed at her discomfort, her eye glued to the scope of her gun, as her partner, Shepard, shifted slightly beside her. They had been lying on the ground for what seemed like hours as they awaited their orders to finally pull the trigger, and they were starting to get uncomfortable on the unforgiving earth. The shifting sound beside her caused her to momentarily take her eyes off of the target. She knew he was only trying to get into a more comfortable position, only to mark their target better, but it still bothered her at how loud he was.

She couldn't help but sigh. Not only did she not like spending hour upon silent hour with Shepard, but she also hated having to await orders from a trigger-shy leader. As great of a leader as William was, he would rather try to talk himself out of a situation or do it without any deaths. However, Shepard and Amariya were people who liked to get things done quickly, which usually meant someone ended up dead, and the damn rocks digging into her armor were about to cause the biggest massacre in the team's history. "These damn rocks…" she started, but Shepard quickly shushed her. *These damn things are causing more discomfort than they should.*

Ugh, it's too cold. She shook her head. *Keep a clear head, James. You've got a job to do and you can't leave it up to Shepard to get it done.*

"Any day now, William," Amariya hissed over their com sets. She was known to be extremely patient, but even the best of them had a breaking point and she was about to meet hers. She was sure that Shepard had noticed how she was starting to flex her hands and shift around on the ground more than usual - obvious signs she was getting antsy.

"I'm still working on getting us in," Jasper, their tech guru, grunted as the sounds of computers beeping and keyboards clacking filled the background. This was the slowest Jasper had taken on opening up any security system to let them in. The IGC must have known they were coming.

"Well, hurry up. This ground is getting uncomfortable," Shepard snapped.

"Don't mind him; he's been crabby ever since we've been here," Amariya piped in with an excuse for her annoying, edgy partner. She couldn't blame him though, even she was getting ready to just say "fuck it" and start shooting.

"I am *not* crabby," he argued back, giving his partner a hell of a side-eye.

"If you're not crabby, then I'm six feet tall," she shot back.

"The more you two bicker, the longer this will take. Now shut up and wait for your mark," William threatened. Their kind-hearted leader never threatened and if he did, he meant it. Both Amariya and Shepard knew that if they pushed enough for him to raise his voice, they had fucked up big time.

"Will all of you stop? I'm trying to concentrate here. Do you know how hard it is to blend in with the Intergalactic Conference? Very hard." TJ, the chameleon of the team, huffed, and then the beeping sound of someone shutting off their com sounded off. Both he and William had found their way into the IGC and were using the opportunity to spy on the head honchos in order to get as much information as possible for the team's employer. The more information the group brought back, the bigger the pay, and the bigger the pay, the happier they were.

"Way to go, guys. You made TJ turn off his com," Jasper teased.

"Will you just hurry it up? It's colder than shit out here," Shepard growled.

"Patience, young one. Breaking into a security system takes time and—"

"Jasper," Amariya hissed a threat to the man, not wanting to listen to his sass while rocks were digging into her ribs.

Their tech sighed at their irritation. Usually, they were able to take his joking around, but tonight was a different story. "I'm in. You're on." He almost sounded hurt about being snapped at, like he was sulking at her harsh tone.

"Finally," Shepard breathed out an annoyed sigh of relief.

"You have your silencer, right, Amariya?" William asked. The man always had to check to make sure everyone had everything they needed and knew what the plan was, even when they had all checked and double-checked before heading out on a mission.

"Yes. And yes, I will make sure to take them out quietly and to not shoot anyone that absolutely doesn't need shot," she retorted. As much as she loved their leader, she wanted him to shut up and just let her do her job.

"And, Shepard, you have…"

"All my knives and stunners. Yes, dear," Shepard sassed at his best friend.

"Try to take as many of the–"

"Guards out without bringing attention to us and clear the way for you guys to get out of there. We'll meet you in Dock

A in an hour," Amariya finished for him. "This isn't my first time."

"Okay, smart ass. And one more thing."

"What's that?"

"Be safe. Both of you." With that, William's line went dead.

"You heard the man. He said to be safe." Shepard chuckled and then put his attention back onto the wall of the main building they had to get into. They had a time limit to get in, get the data, and get the hell out of Dodge, and it was up to him and his partner to get everyone out safely.

"Oh, shit," Amariya cursed under her breath as she spotted an extra piece of security she knew Jasper wouldn't have been able to pick up on the computer system. "Guys, extra security by the main wall. I'm gonna try to take out the power box. Jasper, can you keep the electricity on, and the data room unlocked for us?" she asked over the com.

"Can I keep the electricity on?" Jasper laughed. When no one laughed back, he answered, "I'll work on that. Shoot the box." His line went dead.

"You realize once you shoot that box, we'll be spotted and we'll have to get down there to do everything by hand, right?" Shepard questioned her.

"Hey, as long as you have my back, we'll slaughter the whole house before they know what hit 'em," she answered as she loaded a single bullet into the chamber of her gun. She took in a breath and then released it as her finger tightened ever so slightly around the trigger. With a quick kick of the gun, the bullet launched forward and hit its target. All the lights around the building flickered and then went dark. Loud voices of commands wafted up to the hill as the guards tried to figure out what had gone wrong.

"Party time," Shepard groaned as he stood up and dusted the gravel off of his sleek, black, lightweight armor. He stretched out his arms and neck in anticipation of running down the hill and getting into the physical fight that awaited them. His fighting style forced him to get up close and personal with his opponent, so he needed to be quick and nimble.

"Let's go," Amariya smiled as she slid her gun into its holster on her back. They both ran down the hill and right into the main congestion of guards at the main gate. Shepard started breaking the necks of the guards as Amariya slit their throats and put a bullet in ones that were far beyond their reach. That was the difference between the two. Shepard preferred to use his hands while Amariya used weapons and guns. Despite their differences, they fought together like a well-oiled machine and were extremely effective. It was the perfect dance.

Once they had cleared out the entrance, they casually waltzed into the main building; no alarm had been raised from their attack. "Let's clear the way to the dock and get the flier ready to go as soon as TJ and William get there," Shepard offered as if they had nothing better to do.

"Sure." Amariya shrugged and then went running off towards the docks.

"Are you two in the house?" TJ demanded over their coms. He sounded way more upset than he should have been.

"Yes?" she questioned, as if it wasn't the right answer to give. What could they have done to upset him?

"Shit. I'll try to keep them all distracted. Though when the power flashed, they started getting suspicious. Will, use the key and get into the data room."

"Copy," William said and then cut his line.

"Meet you two at the docks. We'll get a flier and clear the area," Shepard affirmed.

"Amariya. Shepard. You two are closer to the data room than William and TJ. You two would have a better chance to get the data than them if we're to get out before we're found out. I'll run you through it," Jasper chimed in as he watched them from a secure point on the planet. He was the only one not in the firefight as he got to work with the computer systems from far away.

"Son of a bitch," Amariya grumbled. She hated anything that had to do with tech.

"Do you want to be cleared of those charges or not?" Jasper taunted. Ever since they had been accused of conspiring with the Nexxons in order to throw the whole Intergalactic Conference into enough chaos to start a war, they had been working with their current employer to clear their names and find the true culprits.

"Fine. Let's go. Meet you two at the docks," Shepard griped, and they took off. Following Jasper's instructions, they easily found the room and took out guards in the process. They barged into the room and found it surprisingly empty. Only a wall filled with monitors and a few drive docks on the desk were in the small, dark room. "Where is everyone?"

"TJ and William must have distracted them somehow," she guessed just as a loud *boom* rumbled the whole room.

"If they weren't, they are now," he chuckled. Typically, he and Amariya were the ones that caused the distractions, but the other duo was just as capable of blowing shit up when the time came.

"Now, on the desk, there should be a drive dock that is empty. I want you to plug your com into that dock and I'll do everything from there. Got it?" Jasper ordered.

"Got it." Amariya pulled her com from her ear and plugged it in. If it was this easy the whole time, why didn't William or TJ come here in the first place instead of playing spy with the conference?

"How long should this take?" Shepard asked.

"Give me five minutes and I'll have everything we need to prove ourselves innocent," Jasper said.

"I still can't believe we have to prove we aren't in league with Nexxon Galaxy or that they aren't even the ones who blew up the Dome," Amariya grumbled. Just three weeks prior, they had been convicted of treason for helping the Nexxon Galaxy blow up the Dome that the Farron Galaxy did their annual soldier tournaments and ceremonies in. The Intergalactic Conference had actually been the ones to blow it up, and they laid all the blame on William's team because they were the ones who were trying to stop it.

"Got it. You two are good to go," Jasper said. Amariya grabbed her com and placed it back in her right ear.

She now felt more secure knowing she was connected to everyone, especially William. "Are you two at the docks yet?" she asked the two boys on the other side.

"Yes, and we're currently learning how to drive this flier," William answered, sounding as if he was not so sure of the situation.

"This is why you have a chameleon on the team." TJ laughed. While his specialty was geared towards blending into a crowd and being a great spy, it also allowed him to absorb information and new skills quickly. Hence why he was attempting to learn how to drive the flier in such a short amount of time.

"Yeah, still doesn't make me feel better," William quipped back.

"We'll be right there," Amariya chuckled as she and Shepard headed out and towards the docks.

"Halt! Hands where we can see them!" a voice ordered them from behind. They stopped and put their hands on their heads like they were trained. When in a situation like this, it was always easier to make the guards believe they had the upper hand and put them into a false sense of security before striking than fighting them while they were hostile.

"Who are you and why are you here?" another voice asked as the tip of a gun nudged into the small of Amariya's back.

"Well, we're here to kill you. You two especially," Shepard said in a calm voice before he quickly spun around, and his foot connected with the side of a guard's head. The sickening snap of the man's neck breaking filled the air. The second guard let off a spray of bullets just as Amariya flipped a knife out of her boot and sunk it into the man's heart. As the blade pierced the man's armor, a force hit her in the chest and threw her back.

She cried out in pain as she landed hard on her left arm. She grabbed her shoulder and felt the searing pain that came with a dislocated joint. She quickly assessed where she had gotten hit and noticed her fingers came away sticky and red. Not once in her years of being a rogue had she ever been hit with a bullet, and being on the cusp of proving her innocence wasn't exactly the right time to have it happen for the first time. Especially when she knew she was bleeding more than was probably safe. Who was she kidding? It was never safe to actually bleed, no matter the amount.

"For fu–" she started to curse to herself, but the butt of a rifle swung at her. Grunting in pain, she rolled out of the way before it could connect with her skull. Luckily, her right arm hadn't been injured, and she was able to pull her gun from its holster on her hip before shooting her assailant.

Once the excitement of the fight calmed down, she attempted to stand up, but her legs became jelly from the wave of pain that rolled over her. "Shepard," she called over to her partner.

He looked over at her to see the pale look on her face and the awkward angle she was holding her shoulder at. She held up her bloody hand for him to see. The great thing about dark armor was that it kept them hidden in the shadows, but it also meant that bleeding injuries were harder to spot.

Shepard let out a string of curses in his native language of Ze'Levar, the words sounding oddly musical to her ears. "Amariya's been hit. Find a med kit in the flier. We're almost to you guys!" he yelled over the com and picked his small partner up off of the ground, holding her in his arms like a child. If he had the time, he would have wrapped the wound to keep her from bleeding out, but he could hear more guards coming and he wasn't about to stick around to fight them or get caught.

"Easy," she moaned as he jostled her around, sending a shot of pain to her arm.

"Were you hit anywhere else?" he asked, trying to visually assess her.

"Not that I know of," she groaned through bared teeth that were clenched tight from the pain.

"Good." He nodded as he ran through the halls towards the docks. Luckily, she was still able to shoot at the guards that came at them since he was unable to as he carried her. As soon as they reached the flier, William stretched out his arms and took her to him as Shepard turned around to start throwing knives to kill any guards that had followed them. Once he was sure he had gotten all of them, he jumped into the flier and banged on the door to the cockpit. "Let's go!"

"Welcome aboard Air TJ. Please enjoy your flight as we get the hell outta here and back to our freedom. Next stop, Jasper's hiding place." TJ's voice came over the intercom system on the flier. The engines whined, and the craft lifted into the air.

"I've got you," William assured Amariya as he sat her down and started tearing her thin armor off of her so he could inspect the wound.

"I'm fine," she slurred as she tried to push him away from her.

"No, you're not. You could have been killed," he growled. He never liked it whenever one of his team members was hurt while on the job, but he especially hated when Amariya would take one for the team. She never listened to him whenever he told her to be safe and continued to swear by the light armor she wore so that she was light on her feet. Easy to move around in and easy to die in. She was reckless and had a mind of her own, but it was what made her so endearing. He hated it while loving her.

"Hey." Amariya took her com out of her ear. "At least we're free now." A sloppy smile crossed her face.

He sighed as he opened the med kit and pulled out something to start packing her wound to keep her from bleeding out before they got back to their home base. "We're getting you better armor. I can't handle you getting shot again," he warned as he started to wrap her chest to keep pressure on her wound.

"She's reckless. We're lucky she hasn't been shot before." Shepard scoffed as he rolled his eyes.

"All part of the… job." She tried to push it aside as if it were normal, but her voice started to dim.

"You're the shooter, not the target," William couldn't help but argue back. He tied off the wrapping and moved his attention to her dislocated shoulder.

Amariya raised her good arm and placed a hand on his cheek. "You're cute when you're worried."

Shepard couldn't stop the snort that he laughed through his nose at the comment. Apparently, blood loss made her not have a filter on her words. "Cute," he mocked with a quiet chuckle.

William shot the man a warning look before turning his

attention back to the small woman in front of him. "You won't find me cute here in a second," he guessed.

"Wha–" she started, but he grabbed her bad arm and rotated it, quickly popping the shoulder back into place. She screamed at the sudden movement and bit her tongue to keep from cursing the man out. Between the blinding pain and the adrenaline wearing off, she felt her eyes become heavier and her thoughts were starting to become nothing but blackness.

"Sorry," she heard William's voice from a distance.

"That… hurt…" she slurred and slumped her head onto his chest.

"Hey, hold on for me. We're going home. You're not allowed to die on us."

She took in a small breath. "'K."

The last thing she saw was the main building getting smaller and smaller through the opened side door. She finally let the darkness consume her as she dreamed of home and being back in the forest she had grown up in. She dreamed of the wild birds she would hunt and then give her village to help them get by for the week. She dreamed of her brother, whom she hadn't seen since they had arrested him and killed him for treason.

"Welcome home, sis. Like brother, like sister." He smiled at her and held out his hand for her to take.

"Where am I?" she asked, looking around at her surroundings. All around her were tall pine trees and streams of sun poking through bushy branches. It wasn't exactly her childhood forest, but it felt familiar enough.

He simply shrugged. "I promise it's not too bad here."

She reached out her hand.

THE HUNT

H.L. ROBINS

DUST SWIRLED around as the world started to come back into focus and the ringing in her ears dulled to a muffle. Her lungs ached as she sucked in the breath that had just been knocked out of her; she blinked away the stars that swam in front of her eyes. When did she end up on the ground? In fact, how did she allow a demon to get close enough to even put her there? Beth groaned in frustration as she sat up and shook the fog from her head as she coughed away the dirt in her throat.

"It livesss," a gravelly voice hissed behind her.

"Can't say the same 'bout you here in a few minutes," she quipped, rubbing the soreness from the back of her head.

"It ssspeaks." It sounded closer, almost like it was right behind her. Was a demon sassing her?

She reached for the silver knife on her belt, but felt an empty sheath instead. "Shit," she mumbled. Where was her knife? It should have never been knocked from her hand due to the spells she had crafted around it.

"It'sss mine," the demon growled as it lunged at her. She had just enough time to throw herself to the side to dodge the incoming attack and roll onto her feet. The large, burly body of the rancher the demon was inhabiting skidded to a stop and readied itself to jump at her again. Was it the hit to the head messing with her, or was this demon moving faster than it should be able to? Even though they were naturally speedy heathens of hell, they could only move as fast as the body they took up residence in would allow them. And while ranchers had to be pretty quick to run after their wayward livestock, there was no way the massive body of this man could move like that.

"Shit. Shit. *Shit*." If she didn't want to end up as part of the army of the damned, she needed to act fast. Where the hell was her knife? She quickly scanned the area in hopes of catching sight of the silver blade. A glint of metal caught her eye just as the demon launched itself at her. The rune for agility glowed on her left shoulder, just in time for her to bolt out of the way of the new attack. As she tumbled to the ground, she searched for her knife again; the blade flashed in the dimming sunlight. Beth focused magic to the summoning rune on her right hand in hopes of calling the blade to her instead of having to run over to it.

The demon howled with frustration and stomped the ground with a booted foot as it slid right past her. "It *staysss!*" The thing seethed at her as if it were commanding her to stay put before it ran at her once more. First, it sassed at her and now it was throwing a tantrum like a child. What in the world was going on?

When her knife didn't fly into her hand, she let out a string of curses. With no knife, and tired of playing tag, she took her revolver out of its holster and fired a single shot. The demon's head snapped back with the force of the projectile. Its eyes rolled into the back of its head as it rocked back on its heels before falling to the ground with a thud. "'Bout damn time," Beth sighed with a shake of her head.

While using the silver bullets was always easier than trying to get close enough to stab a monster, Beth also hated using them unless absolutely necessary. They were extremely expensive, both monetary and time-wise since she had to carve the runes for the spells she used to make them effective. She holstered her gun and turned to retrieve her knife from where it lay in the short grass.

"That took too damn long," she grumbled to herself as she bent down to pick up her knife. Grabbing it, she studied the blade and noticed why it never came to her. There was a perfectly placed scratch over two of the runes she had carved into it, making the knife impossible to summon and easy to drop. Unfortunately, that meant she would need to scrub all of the runes from it and reapply them.

The hairs on the back of her neck started to prickle as the demon stood up and dived at her turned back. The agility rune glowed once more as she dodged out of the way. She grabbed the lapel of the coat the rancher had been wearing and used the momentum from both of their movements to throw the heavy body to the ground, a cloud of dust erupting around them. She threw herself onto the demon to keep it from trying to get up again.

"This'd be so much easier," Beth raised her silver knife in the air and slammed it into the demon's chest, "if you'd," *stab*, "stayed," *stab*. She raised the knife one last time and gripped it even tighter, whispering the words to activate the enchantments woven into the hilt, the blade turning a bright white. "DEAD." She sunk the knife into the demon's chest once more, the enchantment burning at the dark magic inside the body.

A piercing scream erupted from its mouth and the body disintegrated underneath her, leaving a small piece of sulfur and her silver bullet in its place. Unfortunately, to kill a demon that was taking up residence in a human, she also had to kill the poor soul and destroy the body that was unwillingly taken over. Demons were a nasty business.

Taking a small pouch from her belt, Beth used the tip of her knife to scoop the sulfur into it and sealed the putrid thing away when she pulled the charmed drawstrings. With that done, she sat back on her haunches, taking a breath to stop the wave of dizziness that washed over her and calm down the nerves pulsing through her body. The runes she had activated started to dim and fade back into the white tattooed lines on her arms.

She pushed back the blonde hair that had gotten in her eyes and smoothed a hand down her long braid. Resting her elbows on her knees, she scrubbed her hands down her face in contemplation of what just happened. That fight, no, the whole hunt she had been on had taken too damn long. And the bullet she had lodged in the demon's skull should have killed it on impact. Why the hell did it not kill it? Perhaps Lila, her fellow witch friend, would know something.

Once she was sure she could stand without her legs wobbling like a newborn calf, she got up to gather her coat and hat. She found her black, wide-brimmed hat discarded in a bush not too far from where she had been thrown to the ground and her dark leather duster coat was still piled where she had left it. Dusting both of them off, she put them on and went to her horse. Reaching Rusty, she searched the saddlebags for her canteen of holy water and rinsed the sticky black blood off her blade. As soon as the liquid hit the metal, it sizzled as if the blade was white hot, and the leftover bits of the demon vanished into thin air.

She replaced the knife in its sheath on her belt, stuffed the canteen back in the saddlebag, and hoisted herself into the saddle. "I don't know 'bout you, but I think it's time to call it a night," she muttered to the chestnut as she urged him forward, squeezing her heels at his sides. Rusty seemed to have let out a sigh of relief and agreement as he started on the way toward town. She knew neither one of them wanted to stay out past sundown since there were rumors of a skin-walker skulking around in the badlands outside of town, and she wanted *nothing* to do with it if it was true.

Beth was always grateful that her trusty horse could get her back to town after a hunt, no matter the distance they had traveled previously. Hunts, especially ones handed out to her by Jedediah, always seemed to sap the most energy out of her. It probably didn't help that those assignments always required her to tap into the extra bits of magic she stored away in the runes tattooed along her body.

By the time Rusty got them safely back to Wryridge, the sun was just starting to set and Beth could just make out the shimmer of the Vale, the barrier that split the world into magical and mortal sides, that passed through town. The closer she got, she felt as if she could breathe a sigh of relief as the power of the Vale wrapped around her; there was just something about it that made the very magic in her blood sing in delight.

Once Rusty reached the front of the saloon, Beth climbed off of him and tied him to a post, grabbing her pouch of sulfur bits from her saddle bag. "I won't take long," she told her steed as he stuck his nose in the water trough in front of him and started slurping. "Bite anyone that gets too close." Rusty snored into the water and twitched his ears in response.

"Beth, you're back! I was beginning to get worried." A melodic voice came from down the boardwalk. Beth looked towards the voice and saw her lifelong friend and fellow Noble witch, Lila Crowe. The young woman had long, ankle-length, black hair with purple crocus flowers braided throughout and a natural tan to her skin. Where Beth stored her magic and spells in runes tattooed all over her body, Lila had found a way to use her hair and the flowers as her vessels. Lila was extremely powerful and chose to only leave the Vale when necessary, or in search of new bits of magic. Recently, she had been spending time with one of the local Indian tribes to learn about their nature-based magics and only came to town when she needed something.

The two women embraced in a warm hug before holding each other at arm's length. "Lila! I was actually gonna come see you later. Got a few questions 'bout what's goin' on in the Vale."

A look of confusion crossed Lila's face as she took a step back. "What do you mean?"

"I shot a demon with a silver bullet and it did nothin' to it. How the fuck'd somethin' that powerful get through the Vale?" Beth asked.

Lila shook her head, "The tribe elders I've been living with have mentioned that more and more bad spirits are coming to our plain, but we can't pinpoint why. I've been working with a medicine man to traverse the spirit world to get answers since no one inside the Vale seems to know what's going on."

Beth crossed her arms over her chest and cocked her eyebrows at her friend. "I hope you know what you're doin'. Fuckin' with the spirit world is dangerous. There's a reason I send 'em back."

"I promise that I am being safe. But, Beth, there is so much power in the spirit world and so much to learn! They have shared so much with me. They've shown me what our magic is capable of; that we don't have to have limits if we don't want them." If Beth hadn't been paying attention, she would have easily missed the slight darkness that crossed her friend's face and the way her eyes seemed to lose some of the light behind them. It sent an icy chill down her spine that she wasn't sure how to handle, and she was getting worried about some of the things her friend was saying.

"Just be safe, Lila. Spirit walkin' can lead to some nasty magic and I ain't about to put a blade through your heart if you go dark. There're rumors of a skinwalker out there already, and I don't need you b'comin' one, too." Beth knew that the spirits worked in a quid pro quo manner. They wouldn't give up information or help a mortal on their plain unless they were given something in return. It was how monsters like skinwalkers and demons came about; some poor soul gambled too much and lost themselves to the dark magic.

The other woman gave a small giggle and placed a hand on Beth's shoulder with a smile. "You have nothing to worry about, friend. I'm being safe during my journeys and I have someone to watch over me. The spirits guide me too."

"Good," Beth simply answered with a nod.

"I will be in Wryridge until tomorrow if you wish to continue to talk about your struggle with your demon hunt, but for now, I must continue with my errands." Lila took a step to the side so she could move past Beth.

"Thanks, Lila." With that, the two women parted ways and Beth stepped onto the porch of the saloon and through the swinging doors at the front entrance. As the doors swung closed behind her, she made her way toward Dwight, the barkeep and frontman, who took up his post behind the bar. He was an older man with shoulder-length graying hair, bright blue eyes, and a sun-worn face.

"Lizzie!" He called out over the noise of the room. "Good to see ya back in one piece!" He turned to grab a glass and filled it with two fingers of her favorite whiskey.

Beth sat at the bar and took the glass with a nod of thanks. "Just a simple demon hunt. Nothin' too bad," she shrugged.

"Simple demon hunt," he scoffed. "Ain't no such thing." He gave her a crooked grin.

"Don't know what you're talkin' 'bout," she grinned into her glass.

Dwight let out a barking laugh before he got serious. "Ya look pretty banged up. Must've been a tough one," he commented as he cleaned a glass and filled it for another patron.

Beth glanced into the dirty mirror behind the bar to see what he was talking about. She had a bruise on her left cheek, a good gash across her right eyebrow, and a split lip from the scrape with the last demon. Her blonde hair was frazzled, covered in dust and splatters of dried blood. She nonchalantly waved a hand in front of her face, a hum of magic wafting through the air to clean her skin and knit together the cuts above her eye and on her lip. The rest would have to wait for a bath and sleep. "Won't lie, it was rougher than normal," she admitted.

"But yer alive an' that matters," he raised a glass to her and took a swig.

She couldn't help but roll her eyes at the comment, but she also raised her glass and took a sip. "Some might think otherwise," she mumbled.

"Ya got-" he started, but stopped when she took out her pouch of sulfur bits as proof and dropped it on the bar top.

"You'll find all seven pieces in there and y'all owe me a jug of holy water." She informed him as she took another hit from her drink.

Dwight opened it and poured them out onto the bar top to count out the pieces, using the tip of a knife to push them from one pile to another. "I'll be damned, all seven of 'em."

Beth finished her drink as she waited for Dwight to get her reward money. But when he didn't fish the cash out of the safe behind the bar, she started to get worried. That only meant one thing; Jedediah was holding the reward hostage, and Dwight wouldn't be able to give it to her until she talked to the leader.

"Thanks for the drink, Dwight," she nodded towards him as she placed the glass on the bar top a little harder than necessary.

"Ya gotta see him to get yer money," he told her.

She started to move off of her seat and waved him off. "I don't need–"

"Lizzie, ya need yer money and he's wantin' to see ya." His serious tone never meant anything good.

She stopped her step down, not even looking at him, before replying, "We all want things we can't have."

"Lizzie." He sounded so defeated by her comment.

"Elizabeth," a low, clear voice broke the heavy tension in the room. Everyone's head turned to see Jedediah Wilder standing at the top of the stairs, his arms crossed over his chest, and a permanent scowl on his face. "My office, now."

Everyone turned to look at her to see her reaction. "Rather not, sir," she retorted.

"That ain't an offer," he threw back at her before turning around and heading back to his cave.

"Elizabeth," Dwight's voice came from behind her. The use of her Christian name meant he was urging her to think rationally before she spoke again.

She gave a disgruntled huff and headed up the stairs after the leader of the Grimm Rangers. By the time she got to his office at the end of the hall, he was seated at his desk, looking over a stack of reports from other guild members. Though there were two chairs in front of his desk, she chose to cross her arms over her chest and lean against the door jamb.

"What'd you want, sir?" Beth demanded before Jedediah could launch into some speech about how disappointed he was in her or say something about the latest thing she had done wrong.

He didn't even bother looking up from his stack of paperwork. "It's good to see you too, Elizabeth."

She simply cocked an eyebrow in response.

When she didn't answer back, he set his papers down and looked up at her. "I got another job for you."

"No," Beth shook her head.

It was his turn to cock his eyebrows; like father, like daughter. "What d'you mean no?"

"It means I ain't doin' another job. That last hunt 'bout took everythin' I got."

He sighed and ran a hand through his grey-streaked brown hair. "You'll have time to rest 'fore you go out on this hunt. I'm sendin' Beau out with you and he's still comin' back from his uncle's funeral."

Beth stopped leaning against the door jamb and stood straight at the mention of him. Beau Cartwright was a gunslinger for hire that Jedediah brought in from time to time for some outside help on the more difficult jobs. Beth had worked with him on a few occasions in the past, and the man often joked that they were unofficial partners. The last time she had seen him, they were working together to clear a nest of vampires out of an abandoned mineshaft. If the cowboy turned mercenary was necessary for this hunt, it must have been something serious. Not only did she want to be part of a serious hunt, but she would also never turn down the chance to work with Beau again. He was definitely one of the better partners she had worked with.

"What's the job?" she asked.

"I know you've heard rumors of the skinwalker out in the badlands. They're true, and it's gotten bad 'nough the tribes 'round here want our help to kill it. You 'n Beau are the only ones I trust out there."

If Beth wasn't trying to digest the fact that there really was a skinwalker out there and her own father was sending her out to kill it, she would have reveled in the fact he *actually* complimented her on her skills. She wondered if Lila had an idea about who the Skinwalker was, or if she could do her spirit walking to find the answer. If the monster was real, why had Lila acted as if it were nothing to be concerned about? Perhaps her tribe knew nothing about it? Or maybe she felt safe enough with the medicine man she was working with to not worry about it?

"When'll he be here?" she asked, breaking herself out of her thoughts before they started spiraling.

"Tomorrow, you'll head out in forty-eight hours." At that, he tossed a bag of coin at her. "Payment for your last job." He then tossed another at her. "Get whatever ya might need to be safe. Come back in one piece, will ya?"

She couldn't help but smile, "Yes, sir."

———

Ash and smoke flitted into the nighttime air to dance with the stars as wood was added to a snapping fire. The song of the coyote rang through the valley to create the evening symphony with the frogs, crickets, and other nighttime creatures. The occasional tumbleweed rolled past the camp, startling little nocturnal animals into hiding. A lone deer stalked by the makeshift campsite, just outside the range of the fire's light, causing the traveler's horses to whinny to each other. All in all, it was a rather normal night out on the prairie for the pair of monster hunters. However, normal nights usually set them on edge, never trusting the calmness around them. It didn't help that the Vale didn't feel quite right, and it almost made Beth feel sick.

"What the hell're we waitin' on, Noble? Ain't we

supposed to be huntin', not sittin 'round?" Beau groaned as he juggled a silver dollar between the fingers of his right hand. He always fidgeted with the coin whenever he had the desperate feeling of wanting a cigarette to cut through the stress of a situation.

Beth didn't even bother to look up from the silver bullets she had been etching spell runes into as she let out an exasperated sigh before dropping her voice into a mocking tone. "Nah, I don't gotta know what yer plan is, Noble. We're just huntin' another monster. Don't gotta look at that bounty yer pa gave ya. 'Sides, I can't read." At that, she looked up at him through her long eyelashes to watch his reaction to her words. Even in the dim light of the fire, it looked as if her eyes and the ink in her tattooed spells up and down her arms were glowing.

The man closed his hand around the coin and crossed his arms over his chest. "I can read," he grumbled quietly.

"Wanna read the bounty to me, then?" She continued to stare at him, eyebrow cocked, as a way to double down on her challenge.

Beau stared back at her in hopes that she would back down and just tell him what he wanted to know; their usual song and dance when it came to working together on a job. When she didn't concede, he gave her his signature smirk and flicked the coin with his thumb. "Tell ya what, Noble; heads, ya tell me what we're doin'. Tails, I'll read whatever ya want."

It was her turn to cross her arms over her chest and look at her partner. "Nope, I ain't fallin' for that one again. I know that coin is rigged."

He caught the silver dollar in his hand and placed it over his heart in a dramatic way. "Why, Noble, you wound me so," he winked, his brown eyes shining with humor. It was this boyish humor of his that softened his rugged face and made

Beth remember not to take everything he said or did so seriously.

Beth rolled her eyes and finished etching the rune onto her last bullet. "We're meetin' a friend who might be able to help us." She told him as she inspected the rune and placed the bullet with its friends in the spelled pouch on her belt.

He furled his eyes at her. "Who're we meetin'?"

"If you're patient, she'll be here any minute," she answered cryptically with a nod to the darkness beyond their campfire.

"Le's keep Beau guessin' 'bout what we're doin'. It's so fun," he snarked under his breath as he dug his dagger and whetstone out of his saddle bags and started sharpening the blade. Apparently, flipping the coin had lost its ability to keep his mind focused, and he was in need of something else to do. She had never seen a sharper blade than that of the ones he worked on when he was bored or anxious.

Beth didn't bother to answer him back and decided to simply let him pout. So instead of starting an argument with the man, she took six bullets out of her pouch and carefully placed each one into the chamber of her revolver, whispering spells to connect the runes on the bullets and the gun to each other. If they were going to be taking on a skinwalker, she wanted to make sure she took every precaution available and be ready for anything to happen. It definitely helped that everything they hunted was easily taken down by silver and the element also held magic nicely.

A mutual silence washed over the campsite as the two hunters went about their busy tasks. Beau continued to sharpen his knives and Beth loaded and reloaded her gun, making sure the spells were intact. Eventually, the sound of crunching gravel gave notice to someone coming closer to their campsite. A slight hum of magic alerted the witch to who their visitor was.

"Thanks for comin', Lila," Beth called to the darkness as if there was someone out there.

The long-haired witch stood right outside of the firelight, the crocus flower pedals casting enough of a shadow to cover their purple color. Her dull eyes now looked almost lifeless and her skin was a paler color than normal. And was there a hint of blood on her hands? The protective circle seemed to shimmer in front of her like a barrier. "Beth," she nodded to her friend.

Beau looked between the two women as if he was trying to figure out how to handle the situation. "Who's this?" he finally asked.

"This is Lila, the friend I told you 'bout." There was a sense of caution in her voice as she introduced him to the other witch. There was something off about her and Beth didn't like it. She should have been able to step up to the barrier without it triggering that it was there.

"The one who'll help with the hunt?" He seemed to catch onto his partner's cautious tone as he, too, sounded unsure.

Lila's head snapped to look at the gunslinger and then back at the other witch, the angles and speed almost unnatural. "Hunt?" she asked, anger seeping through her tone. The woman took a step back from the camp as if she were readying her escape.

Shit, Beth thought to herself. She had hoped that she could have invited Lila into the circle to capture whatever she was sure had attached itself to her friend, so she could exorcise it before it truly took her over. Once she had saved her friend, she was going to ask her to help them actually hunt the skinwalker they had been sent to find, since she knew they needed extra power for something like that. She was also silently cursing Beau for not paying attention to her when she went over the plan the first time. He wasn't supposed to let Lila in on the fact they were there for a hunt. When she had asked her friend to join them earlier, she had simply mentioned they were in need of help finding herbs and other ingredients that could only be found at night since she was so versed in them.

"Yeah, Beau, this's the friend who's gonna help us get things we need for our hunt that we're goin' to after t'night." Hopefully, he was able to catch onto what she was saying without making it too obvious.

He narrowed his eyes at her and then snapped his fingers as if he remembered. "Right. She's here to help get those night critters and plants we need."

At this, Lila seemed to release the tension in her shoulders and softened the scowl on her face. "So, you're not hunting now?" she asked.

Beth couldn't help but let out a snorted laugh. "I'm always huntin'. C'mon over and we'll talk 'bout what we need." She motioned with a scoop of her arm for her friend to join them around the fire.

The other woman shook her head and planted her feet where they were. "No, we must get started now if we're to gather everything we need."

The hunter gritted her teeth at her friend's refusal. She needed her to walk into the circle before she went anywhere with her out there in the dark. She always had people go through a protective barrier if she had either never met them or had a weird feeling about them. She had even had Beau walk through one earlier, since they hadn't seen each other for a few weeks. "Walk up to the fire, Lila," Beth demanded through her clenched teeth, trying to keep the annoyance out of her voice.

"No," the witch refused with another shake of her head. "You need to come with me so we can get started. We - I don't have much time."

"I ain't leavin' this fire 'til you come over here. I know ya feel that magic circle 'round me and ya know I gotta make sure you're safe 'fore I go anywhere with you," Beth tried to reason with her.

"No."

"Dammit, Lila. Get your ass up here."

"NO!" Lila's voice sounded as if it had dropped a few decibels and her eyes flashed red. A blast of power radiated off of her as she boomed her answer. The blast was enough to scare the horses into snapping their reins off of the posts they were tied to so they could run off. It also flattened the few shrub brushes that were around the campsite and pushed small rocks and timber away. However, the force did not permeate the circle Beth had put up. With the force of power, Lila's form melted into that of a scraggly-looking coyote and she took off towards the ravines and spires of the badlands. Wanting to hide from them, no doubt.

"The hell?" Beau yelled as Beth groaned, "For fuck's sake." The two grabbed their weapons and took off running after Lila. Thank goodness for the full moon to help them see their way through the dark.

"The fuck is that thing?" he demanded of her as they came to the first spire and Beth motioned for them to flatten themselves against it.

She pulled out her revolver and cocked the hammer. "That's what we're here for," she hissed back as she looked around the formation to see if anything was in front of it.

"Which is?" he led.

She turned her head to look at him. "A skinwalker. It's a demon inside the body of a witch. I fuckin' told her to be careful. Go 'round that way and see if you can catch her from behind. I'll keep her distracted." She pointed to the upper ledge of the rock formations. He simply nodded and did as he was told.

"Beth," a voice sang out to her and echoed through the

ravines. It sounded like a mixture of her friend's voice and something darker, more powerful.

"What the hell did you get yourself into, Lila?" she answered back. She shuffled around the spire to look across the small ravine. In the moonlight, she watched the shadow of a coyote shift and morph into that of a deer.

"I found power, Beth. I can speak with our dead. I have no bounds now." The deer shifted again; the sounds of snapping bone bounced off of the valley walls as the form began to stand upright. Beth moved to be out in the open in hopes of keeping the skinwalker's attention on her so that Beau could get where he needed to without being caught. The monster quickly caught sight of her and started staggering towards her. Each step looked painful, as if the knees and hips of the deer body couldn't fully move the way it wanted them to. Its red eyes seemed to glow in the sockets of a rotting deer skull, bits of flesh slipping and sliding off the bone.

It lunged at her with unnatural speed. She shot at the thing as it got closer, the hole where the bullet it glowed an angry silver color. She then dove behind another spire to get out of its way. "Why d'ya gotta talk to the dead, Lila? Let them be," she called over her shoulder as she cocked the hammer once more. One bullet down, five to go.

"We have answers, Beth. I can teach you what you need to know. I can tell you why I died," the voice sounded eerily like her mother's.

She so badly wanted to ask a question that only her mother knew the answer to, but she knew the skinwalker was only playing with her. But, spirits, if it wasn't hard to hold her tongue so she could hear her mother's voice one more time.

"Elizabeth," the soothing voice of her mother reached her ears as the creature moved closer to her.

Beth ran across the ravine to the spire on the other side, letting off two more bullets into the monster. As the bullets hit their mark, a horrific scream sounded through the night. The magic in them must have been doing something right, as she could smell sulfur coming from the wounds. In the moonlight, she also noticed the animal parts were starting to fall off, and the body was looking more human. She took in a deep breath and eyed the next spire she needed to move to in order to get the skinwalker close enough for Beau to jump out and get it from behind.

"Fuck off!" she yelled out to the night.

A clawed hand swiped at her just as she dove from behind the spire and made a move for the one she needed to get to. It caught her by the back of her duster coat and threw her to the ground. It readied itself to jump on her, but a holler from behind them distracted it as Beau jumped off of the cliff edge, silver dagger pointed at its back. The monster quickly spun around, catching the gunslinger midair, holding him by the throat. Its hand started to squeeze the air out of him and his eyes began to roll back in his skull. He dropped the dagger in his hand and it clattered away from him.

"No!" Beth cried out. She pointed her revolver at the back of the creature and fired her last two rounds into it. With each hit, it loosened its grip on Beau until he dropped to the ground in an unconscious heap. Now that it was full of magic from the bullets, the creature was no longer able to hold its animal-like appearance and now looked just like Lila but now with six wounds that glowed silver. Though it looked like her friend, she knew the demon was still in control.

The skinwalker bent down to start attacking the unconscious body of Beau, but Beth was able to scramble off of the ground and jump onto its back. With the force of the move, she pushed the creature away from him and to the ground. The two former friends wrestled on the solid earth of the ravine, the once beautiful flowers in Lila's hair becoming crushed under them. Both of them were able to land a few punches on the other and the demon inside Lila started to get the upper hand as it made a move to pin Beth to the ground.

"Join me, Daughter Noble. Together we can have all of the power," the voice of the demon spoke through Lila's mouth. Its hand wrapped around her throat and started to squeeze the air out of her.

"Go to hell," she groaned, her vision going dark.

"Then you shall go with me," it cackled as it tightened its grip.

Just as she was about to fade, the hand released her throat, and the weight was gone. "Get up, Noble!" She heard Beau's voice from a distance. She shook her head and her voice cleared. She saw that he had stuck his dagger into Lila's shoulder and threw her to the ground.

Before Lila could get up, the runes of Beth's body glowed to give her the strength to jump up and pin her former friend to the ground. As she did so, she felt a subtle change in the magic around them.

"Please, Beth. Do it." It was Lila's voice and eyes that begged her friend to stick the dagger in her chest to end her life. "I'm so sorry. I just wanted to learn. I wanted to know!"

Beth gripped the handle of the silver dagger in both her hands and raised it above her head. "I'm so sorry, old friend. May you find peace in the afterlife and find our sisters for comfort." With that, she brought the blade down and plunged it in Lila's heart as she spoke the enchantment to activate the spells etched in the silver. As the blade touched her heart, a white light poured out of the wound and bloomed all around them. Both Lila and the demon inside of her screamed with pain as the darkness burned away from inside of her. Beth wanted to let go of the blade and try to stop the torture, but she knew she couldn't. The only way to kill a demon was to kill the body it resided in as well.

Lila's body disintegrated underneath her, leaving a piece

of sulfur and one of her crocus flowers. Beth dropped the blade and shoved her face in her hands as a sob erupted from her chest. She mourned the loss of her friend, the idea that she had heard her mother's voice, and the betrayal she had felt from someone she had been so close with. She heard Beau's footsteps as he approached her and was grateful that he had chosen to stand there and give her all the time she needed to compose herself.

"Ready?" he asked.

She didn't answer. She simply got up and followed him out of the ravine and into the sunrise.

THE DOOR THROUGH THE HALLOW TREE

H.L. ROBINS

You see,
there's this strip of woods made
of hedge, elm, hack, and redbud
that follows the little creek behind
the old blue farmhouse.
The trees are old, worn,
full of thorns,
and quite honestly
look like they belong
in a horror movie.
The branches and gnarled bark
are dark with age.
The ground is bare of grass
and worn by trampling feet.
But above,
they are a sea of green in the spring
and catch fire in the fall.

But this place is more than just nature
at work, it's where imagination is

put to the test.
Where things are not
what they seem and yet
it's everything
at the same time.

There's this particular looking
tree that splits in two
with branches that curve
and hang low to the earth.
Its placement is the perfect entrance
to a whole
new
world.
As you walk through,
you leave behind a pig farm in Kansas
and enter a place
where your imagination is the only
limitation.

One day,
it's a magical forest
where the trees become sentient
and you are a knight
wandering through
to make it back to your kingdom.
The fallen branches you gather
have now become swords
to slay the dragons that fly above
and the monsters on the ground.
The sounds of the fluttering leaves
are whispered secrets
flying in the wind
between your towering friends.

The fallen leaves, thorns, and hedge apples
become parts of a magic spell
or potion mixed in the large, rusty pot
found in the old trash heap.

Another,
it is a desolate planet
and you're there to explore it.
The pigs that inhabit the space
are the enemy and aliens
that you must hide from.
Those same sticks from before become
ray guns or sabers to defend
yourself and those around you.
The empty space between
the creek bank and bent
tree roots make for the perfect
place to hide away from the aliens.
Hedge apples are now eggs,
bombs, or poisonous spores.

Though it is a small swatch of land,
and the creek is rarely filled
with running water,
it is so much more than
it appears.
The piles of old tires and
kitchen appliances are easy to
hide behind and explore.
They're not junk.
They're tactically placed to
slide down the muddy bank
and spy out at the aliens
or whatever else those pigs

might be that day.
The jars, bottles, and old pots
are filled with muddy water as "provisions"
for the next adventure.
 Rusty tin sheets and wooden boards
are spliced together against
clumps of trees and tall roots
to make a shelter or castle.

The door through the tree hollow
is not just the way to get into
the hedge row or to the creek
trickling from the big pond.
It is the entrance to a world
as big as your imagination.

————

ROBINS GREW up on a farm and continues to live the small town life with their three fur-babies and partner in southeast Kansas where they work for a local college. From writing their own versions of "The Black Lagoon" books in elementary school to working on full novels and a book of poetry, Robins has been in the creative writing space most of their life. While in university, they had short stories and poems published in the institution's literary magazine. Robins tends to pull from all sorts of media, from high fantasy and science fiction to westerns and comedy, while writing and compiling ideas for new worlds to create. Robins is an avid DnD player and enjoys going to concerts for independent rock bands.

FIRE IN THE BLACKFELL MOUNTAINS

C. W. STEVENSON

THE STENCH of the creature might have been the foulest thing Svern had ever endured in his sixteen years, like a mixture of wet dog and sulfur. The carcass of the dragon lay with its guts exposed to the men where Grom had splayed it open. Alive, the creature had been the size of a large horse. Dead, it had shriveled considerably.

Svern looked up at his father. "It's small," he observed, poking at an open rib with a stick.

Around them, boulders and shrubs littered the terrain of the Black Fell Mountains, save for a few birch and pine trees scattered about. Further up, basalt covered the mountain side, its dark color a testament to the mountain range's namesake.

"It's a juvenile Roundhorn," Grom corrected him. "Yras is adamant a more impressive specimen is at large. But it is no matter. This one will do."

"Rare, no? A Roundhorn in these parts?" Allos asked.

"Rare enough," Grom said as he scanned the surrounding mountain peaks, causing Svern to do the same.

His father's sense of uneasiness was enough to question whether his father *truly* believed this was the beast that had plagued the region's countryside. Perhaps it didn't matter. After all, they just needed to kill a dragon, not *the* dragon. That had been the arrangement between the marshal, Grom, and the others in their party. Once proof of a dragon's demise was brought to the marshal, the hide, bones, and claws were theirs to sell to the highest bidder.

On this slope of the mountain, the ground wasn't so steep. They'd made camp in this frigid land after Yras and Grom had come across dragon scat and rub signs on the trees where a Roundhorn had been marking its territory. The tracks they'd discovered had been large.

Larger than this pitiful creature.

Svern had stayed behind the cover of nearby boulders while Grom and Allos had cornered the thing, killing it with two well-thrown spears before it could take flight. Svern hadn't protested. He wasn't his father, however much he wanted to be, or *pretended to be*. He hadn't killed a dragon before. Grom the Red had slain an adult Thornback when he'd been sixteen.

After the Roundhorn had taken its final breath, they had hauled the creature back to camp on a makeshift travois where they would take its skin for coin, provide the horns to the marshal, and pack the meat for the journey home. Then, they could return to their farms with their lives and a few coins richer while the war raged on.

Svern could think of worse outcomes. The dragon *could* have been larger.

Allos clutched the wolf-skin cloak closer to his body. "Blast this wind. Might've taken my chances on the front lines if I'd known what awaited us."

Join the fighting in the Hipani deserts… or join the hunt.

Grom had explained to Svern their choices, a choice Svern would have to decide for himself as a man grown.

He'd repeated his father's words to the marshal, of

course. He'd no wish to die on the front lines—just another pointless war between disgruntled kings. But there wasn't a soul alive who dared name them cowards. To hunt a dragon in lieu of military service... few would see it as the safer alternative.

But to hunt two? Svern feared the others would only see the coin they stood to gain rather than the danger the idea proposed. Dread washed over him at the thought of facing such a beast. A juvenile had been bad enough.

Continuing the lesson, Grom knelt down and sliced the dragon from its sternum up to its chin. Parting the meat and sinew, he gestured down for Svern to look.

"See there?" Grom began. "Pyroctic sacs on either side of the esophagus. These glands are how these bastards produce fire." Grom held out his knife. "Here."

Taking the bone-handled hilt in his grasp, Svern knelt beside his father.

"Stab one of the glands," his father instructed.

Svern wondered if his grandfather had done the same for his father the first time he'd been close enough to a dead dragon. It reminded Svern of his first deer. His father had taught him how to gut, skin, and quarter it, no doubt the way *he'd* been taught as a boy—skills passed down from generation to generation. There was nothing glorious about dead things, but to waste a thing because one did not wish to bloody their hands was not the way.

Svern did as he was bid. Slowly, he inched the tip of the blade until he heard a soft *hiss* emit from the sac. His eyes widened as smoke leaked out from the tiny slit. Svern shuffled backwards on his knees, pulling his hands back toward his body.

Grom smiled. "It can do no harm."

Allos laughed from his place next to the fire. "I think it's dead, lad!"

Svern ignored him. Looking back at his father, he asked, "Then how does it breathe flame if not from the glands?"

"It does not. Dragons ingest a great many minerals, much of it coating their teeth. When the vapor is secreted through the glands and enters the mouth, the minerals and vapor together make fire."

"What minerals do they ingest?"

"Many. It is not known if it is a mixture of several types of mineral deposits or one in particular."

Svern and his father got to work then. They gutted the creature, skinned, and quartered it. Svern swatted at flies as his father guided his hand throughout the process. His father didn't seem to mind. Around death, Svern thought his father looked as calm as if he were drinking a pint beside their hearth. Some men were just numb to violence and what it wrought on account of the violence they had experienced or had wrought down upon others. His father was one of those people.

Svern was not.

After they'd washed the blood from their hands, Svern's father patted him hard on the back. The power from just one hand nearly sent Svern a few steps forward. He rubbed at the sting as his father looked out across the moors.

"All in a day's work, eh boy?" Grom asked. "Come now, we'll throw some of this meat on the fire while it's fresh. You've never had dragon when it's like this. Allos, make yourself useful and cook this."

Allos stood up then, undoubtedly prepared to give the usual vulgar retort, when his smile quickly faded away. "Quiet," Allos said to them, raising a hand in the air for silence.

Svern listened to their surroundings. A crow cawed, but it was far off. There was only the sound of his own sudden heavy breathing.

Then he heard it.

Footsteps approaching, crunching across the frozen grass and rocks. Getting closer.

"Father," Svern said, motioning to the west.

From the path they'd left, Garen and Yras suddenly appeared. By the look of them, they were exhausted, sweating, even amidst the freezing cold.

"What happened?" asked Grom.

"Saw'm," Yras gasped. Taking a moment to catch his breath, he continued. "Big fucker. Ten hands *at least*. This one's kin I wager."

Garen began packing his things into his possibles bag, long curls of blond hair and an even longer beard blowing with the mountain breeze. He looked up at Grom, then to Allos, and Svern. "Move it. He's flown around to the east side of the mountain. Pack."

"Must we?" Svern heard his father ask.

Garen stopped what he was doing. "Must we what?" he asked.

"We've got one dead already. We could head back now, and none would be the wiser."

The scowl on Yras's face was one Svern knew well. He'd worn it much of the journey. Perhaps it was the cold accentuating his expression, but the look on the man's face made him appear ready to do murder.

"And what happens when there is a dragon seen snatching livestock, and then *people*? What then?" Yras was fuming now. "Will the law understand you hadn't the gall to hunt it down? We will be beheaded for cowardice, or worse!"

"We *have* a dragon! For the sake of the gods, man, my son travels with us."

Yras scoffed at that. "*Grom the Red*," he said, shaking his head. "Grom the *Yellow* is more befitting to your talk." He looked at Allos. "What about you? You would pass up the chance for a skin so large it would keep our purses heavy with coin for the next few crop yields?"

Allos said nothing as Grom walked toward the smaller man.

To say Grom was large was an understatement. Svern was a man grown, but his father's weight doubled his own and stood a head taller. Yras's cold, brave look quickly gave way to fear as the known killer stopped at an arm's length away.

Grom sized Yras up and shrugged. "You would trade your life for blood money? If the beast is as large as you say, it will be no easy feat."

"You've done in a brute like this once before," Yras pointed out.

"Aye," Grom said. "And I'm telling you, *all* of you, we should head back. Tell no one of a second. We return home with our spoils and return to our wives. You'll live longer this way. I can promise you that."

Garen spoke up. "No. There are five of us to outwit the beast. It cannot withstand so many spears."

Grom turned to Allos. "Allos?"

Allos furrowed his brow. "Mmm. It would be a great deal of coin, Grom."

Svern had heard enough of Allos' constant talk of brothels to know the thing driving the man's thought process.

"And you, son?"

Svern was surprised by his father's words. When he looked around, he saw that the others were waiting for his response. If he said no, he was sure they would return home. But the others would see him for what he was—a scared boy. Svern couldn't have that. The son of Grom the Red was no coward. The son of Grom the Red did not back down from a dragon, from man, beast, or danger of any kind. He welcomed it with a smile.

And so, Svern, son of Grom the Red, bent down by his bedroll, and took up his axe.

———

A twig snapped beneath Svern's feet.

Yras looked back, placing a finger to his lips.

Ghyrzia, hear my prayer. Please… grant me your strength. He doubted she was listening. The Goddess of the Hunt, of Mercy, and Storms had far more important things to worry about than his worthless carcass.

Why he'd insisted they continue on with the hunt, he wasn't so sure any longer. With all eyes on him, in that moment, it'd felt like the only choice.

Svern grimaced.

My decision. Time to see it through.

After breaking camp, Grom had doused them all with the juvenile Roundhorn's urine.

"To cover our scent," his father had said. "We want this beast to be at ease upon approach."

Svern understood perfectly—an unsuspecting dragon was less prone to bathe them in flame.

He wasn't sure if his father had seen his trembling legs. Svern had done his best to squash his fear for what lay ahead, but it left him feeling hollow, as if his guts were replaced with bile. "How would the adult not know its young is dead? Can it not smell it?"

"The rot has not set in. But soon enough my son, yes, the scent of death will send this creature into a rage we would not want to be within a hundred leagues of."

They had traversed the mountainside, passing amongst the trees and larger boulders for cover. Their destination was not far. The further they traveled along the base of the mountain, the more dragon sign lay scattered about; a birch half shaven near the top where it'd rubbed its horns, a mound of scat, dry scales that'd come away whilst basking in the sun, and finally, tracks.

Svern had never seen anything like it.

As the others circled around the first track, he counted the imprint where six clawed toes had embedded themselves into the ground.

"There should be seven," Grom whispered.

"What does it mean?" asked Garen.

"It means… it has faced man before and lived."

"Soon enough, the brute shall have fewer limbs still," bragged Yras.

Garen gave no reply. The look of concern washing over his face was enough to tell what the man was feeling. The prospect of facing a *mature* Roundhorn who'd tasted man-flesh was nothing to look forward to. Svern wondered how much of Yras's courage would remain when they came face-to-face with the beast.

"Quiet," Grom said over his shoulder. "All of you." His father pointed up ahead. "The trees, look."

Not far in the distance, what few trees remained were missing their greenery, and branches as well. A few dozen in all, most stood erect while some had fallen, cracked near the base.

"Rub marks?" asked Svern.

"Aye," replied Grom, his tone grim and ominous. It wasn't often he saw his father so unnerved.

Allos sighed. "Why did it use so many trees? Could there be more than one adult?"

"There is only one," Grom replied. "And it's a *she*."

Svern winced at the jerk of the other's heads, all turning to look at Grom, as if he'd uttered a curse on the very ground they walked. A valid concern when considering a female was far more dangerous. She'd be fighting not just for her own life, but that of her offspring as well.

Grom explained, "Before laying the eggs, the horns of a female began to ache more as they shed." He led them further on until they stopped at the first fallen tree. "She was in great pain."

"Was?" asked Allos.

Grom nodded his head. "Mmm," he grunted. "Was. This tree fell some time ago. The juvenile was the last surviving offspring from her previous clutch of eggs." Grom went to his knees. Putting his nose to the earth, he sniffed like a hound. He took a handful of loose soil, letting it fall in between his fingers before using the butt of his spear to help prop him to his feet. He met each of their eyes, his gaze landing on Svern last. "We are close."

"How do you know?" Svern asked.

Grom glanced down. Svern followed Grom's eyes until he saw it. Broken soil and rock trailed up the mountain as if a trench had been started, but never finished.

Tail tracks.

Grom took point once more. His extra spear jutted from where it was tied to his pack. The other, he held out in front, the spearhead aiming at the mountain's peak, white knuckles beginning to show as he gripped the shaft tighter.

Remaining close behind his father, Svern followed his stride step-for-step as they began the journey back up the mountain. But it was the tail markings which served as their guide now.

Svern didn't bother glancing back at the others. Their fear wouldn't be unlike his own. But his father? His fear was one of caution, not just out of respect for the awesome power of the Roundhorn, but for *him.*

Eyes glued to his father's back, he followed.

————

Basalt rocks began to sprout from all around the hunting party the further they trekked. As individual clusters of rock turned into meandering walls, the men did their best navigating through the black maze. Oftentimes reaching a wall of rock blocking their path, they would simply turn around and follow another path. This instance was no different.

His father turned to face them. Gesturing with a finger pointing at his nostrils, the entire party began to sniff.

A new stench had grown as they followed the tail markings, growing stronger when the markings had vanished. He'd smelt it before.

Wet dog… sulfur.

The juvenile had carried the odor, but only slightly. In this place, with black rock surrounding their view, they all knew what they would find in the end.

Following a new path, the smell grew in intensity. Svern spotted an opening, the exit to their rocky maze. Trepidation summed their gait as they stepped into open ground, their weapons at the ready.

Svern was sure to steer carefully around the dragon's leavings—bits of beasts and men still decomposing, but mostly bone. Flies swarmed around them, though no man risked swatting. Any sudden movement, clatter of bones, a cough, a whisper—it could all mean a fiery end.

He watched his father crouch low, the first sign that he was stalking his prey.

Svern and the others emulated his movement. As Svern realized they were headed toward another wall of black rock, he began to wonder where his father was leading them. Heart thumping, his throat dry, and sweaty hands gripping a spear, Svern scanned the area.

Nothing.

Breathing a sigh of relief, Svern relaxed his shoulders. Then, the wall of rock moved.

————

The Roundhorn let free a terrifying snort, creating a small cloud of dust near its nostrils, holes so large Svern thought his head might fit perfectly inside one of the dark cavities.

It continued to sleep, heaving in deep breaths in and exhaling out, each time creating another small dust cloud.

His father whispered to them all as they came together to devise a plan. He looked at Garen first. "You and me are climbing the hill behind the bastard."

"What? Why?" Garen asked, his voice full of concern, as if the very notion was unfair, no matter the strategic reason behind the order.

"To rain spears down on its head, you dolt." Grom turned to Svern then, eyeing the others in turn after. "If it wakes, distract it."

Yras nodded.

Allos looked unsure.

Svern… began to breathe heavily.

"No, no, no," he muttered, the words coming out in a panic. But at least he had sense enough to speak quietly in his most untimely outburst. "It's going to bloody *kill us!*"

Grom shook his head. "No," he said sternly. "I—" he looked back to Garen, "*We* are going to kill the damned thing. But you and the others will see we are given the time to do it." Grom gripped his spear in a fighting stance. "*Thrust!*" The spear shot out, the spearhead whipping through the air before being pulled backward. Grom got into a throwing position. "Aim for the chest, neck, or head. You've all got three spears. Make them count, eh?"

Yras was looking at Grom as if he were Savage the Black

come back from the dead. He grinned madly. "*Yes!*" he growled.

Allos gave a weak smirk and looked at his old neighbor, Grom the Red, the legendary warrior next door who'd convinced him to come along with him and his son. From the man's expression, it was little wonder to Svern if Allos had also contemplated if he'd made the right choice in following Grom's decision to escape the war.

Only the outcome could tell. One thing was for certain: they *were* about to face a foe beyond any one of them.

In the end, Allos gave a sharp, "Aye, alright then."

Then they were off.

Garen took off to the left, while Grom took off to the right. They circled around the dragon, partially hidden by the amount of fallen boulders for an uncomfortable few moments until both came into full view from behind the beast.

The two men edged closer, coming down the slope of the mountain that would put them directly over the Roundhorn's tail, only twenty strides from each other's position. Svern gritted his teeth at each step his father took. One misstep, and Grom would come rolling down the mountain, alerting the beast to their presence.

The Roundhorn's nostrils flared open as it exhaled again, every breath that came through those black pits proving the truth, that this monster was *real*, in front of him, and every bit as terrifying as his father had made a full-grown dragon sound. He'd heard the stories: how his father had slain a dragon of monstrous proportions when he'd been around Svern's own age. Men loved to boast of his father's deeds, bought him drinks in the tavern, had bought *Svern* a tankard or two just for being the spawn of a hero. Every man wanted to be *Grom the Red*.

Looking at his father now, Svern didn't want anything less than for his father to sneak back down, gather their gear, and return home to his mother, his sisters, to their fields. What he wouldn't give to smell that faint sweet smell of barley in the early morning, to enjoy a meal sitting at the table with his family rather than sit around the campfire another night, or the constant fear of the unknown as each day had brought them closer to this very moment.

But Grom the Red couldn't come down from that mountain slope any more than Svern could turn and abandon his father and the others to their fate. It wasn't the way.

Better to die a hero than face the shame of living the life of a coward. He used to believe those words… words he'd heard from every man worth their salt in a fight, from his father especially. Now, with the threat of danger so close, he wondered if all the dead heroes wouldn't mind trading places with the living cowards of the world. Svern knew what he would choose.

The crashing of rock made Svern feel like his lungs would drop into his stomach. He didn't dare breathe. He'd been so keen on watching his father's footsteps, that he'd completely ignored Garen.

Svern watched in horror as Garen yelped. One of his spears clattered to the ground, right beside the dragon's head, the butt of the weapon actually touching skin as it came to a halt.

The Roundhorn groaned lazily as it picked itself up. It grew bigger with each passing second, *much bigger* than Svern could have dreamed an animal could or *should* get, for that matter. The stuff of nightmares rose higher and higher. Deep yellow eyes glared down upon Svern and the others before it turned its head to see Garen struggling in his attempt to keep himself from rolling further down.

It didn't move fast, it didn't even growl. There was no roar of ferocity as Svern had expected given the circumstances of being woken up from what'd been a deep sleep. Instead, the

Roundhorn casually turned its body to face the now screaming form of Garen as he came to realize what was about to become of him. Its neck stretched to one side before coming down as if to pop its neck, then the jaws opened and when they came back up, the bottom half of Garen was falling to the ground. There was a loud *slap* as Garen's remains hit the rocks below.

Svern was about to turn and ask Allos what they should do when the battle cry of Grom the Red echoed across the mountainside.

He watched in awe as his father leapt into the air, spear pointed downward, his teeth clamped together so hard and eyes bulging so wide that he hardly looked like the same man to Svern. The Roundhorn remained impassive, seemingly unconcerned with his father, another fly amongst hundreds more. But things quickly changed as Grom's spear stuck through the beast's bulging neck.

Grom rolled masterfully as he met the surface, yelling "Spear!" and held his hands out.

Allos tossed Grom one of his spears and readied to throw the next. Then the Roundhorn's tale came whipping in from the side. Catching Grom across the chest, the force of impact sent him flying a couple dozen yards away.

"Kill it!" Allos screamed at Svern and Yras.

Allos' spear hit rock, somehow missing the dragon entirely.

By that time, Yras and Svern both had a spear flying through the air. They lodged close together, both spears penetrating the dragon's neck once again. Now three spears stuck through flesh. Dark blood was gushing out fast now, running down from neck to chest before raining to the ground, red droplets pitter pattering against the rocks.

Now the Roundhorn roared, an otherworldly sound so terrible that Svern quit moving. He was frozen in place again, legs unable, or unwilling, to move. Through his peripherals, he saw Allos throw down his remaining spear and run for the maze of rocks.

"The *neck*, lad, aim for the neck!"

It was Yras, his voice snapping Svern out of his moment of fear. Svern was just preparing to hurl his second spear when the fire came.

Yras's fiery shape went charging at the Roundhorn, spear-point raised. But the pain must've become too much because the next thing Svern saw was Yras diving to the ground screaming, rolling, and writhing with panic at the flames eating away his clothes, his flesh. The Roundhorn breathed another fiery spray, this time with enough force and close proximity that Yras ceased to be.

Ashes to the wind.

The Roundhorn bent its neck upward, releasing a plume of excess grey fumes toward the sky.

Svern closed his left eye, picking the place on the Roundhorn's bleeding neck where he wanted the spear to go, feeling that special place in his throwing arm. He'd hit it once, a true strike. It couldn't take another. The weight of the spear was well balanced in his grip. Skipping forward to let loose the spear, Svern slipped, a bloody rock ruining the moment, *his* moment for his place in the songs told 'round the fire.

Stumbling to the ground, he didn't wonder what they would have called him had he succeeded in killing the beast, only how much his death would hurt. He waited to feel jaws clench around his midsection, serrated teeth entering flesh like so many knives, to feel the crunching of his bones before he went sliding down the back of the Roundhorn's gullet. Or maybe it would be the flames for him. *Ashes* like Yras.

The dragon approached, jaws widening as it closed in the short distance, the earth shaking Svern's body with each step.

Svern closed his eyes.

I am sorry, father. Mother.

His father's battle cry filled the air and Svern's eyes burst open. Grom the Red, Slayer of Dragons, and Bane of the Battlefield came flying down from the wall of rock once more. Dagger in hand, Grom thrust the point down onto the Roundhorn's skull.

It roared, shaking its head wildly, all three spears in its neck becoming dislodged in the chaos, causing one of the bloody spears to clatter down in front of Svern.

"Spear!" screamed Grom, holding onto the hilt of his dagger for dear life.

The Roundhorn snapped its jaws, desperately trying to catch one of Grom's dangling legs. Fire came spewing from its mouth again, the impact of the flames causing rock and debris to fly, creating a cloud of dust and smoke.

Springing to his feet, Svern took the bloody spear in hand. There was no fear. No more frozen legs or the thoughts of agony to come… only the task at hand. *Kill the dragon.*

 Risking a second to wipe the slippery mass of red oozing down the shaft, all Svern accomplished was smearing the dragon's blood down further. Still, he did not falter.

Svern aimed, reared his throwing arm back, came forward in three long strides, and released.

The world around him slowed to a near halt as the lives of him and his father were carried along on the point of a spear. The Roundhorn emitted a high-pitch screech as the spear hit true, burying itself beside the other bleeding holes.

Massive yellow eyes fluttered, and the dragon lurched forward. It roared. Not powerful like before… but weak, spent.

Svern was just about to turn and run when the dragon came crashing to the ground. A deep breath in, a final exhale, and the Roundhorn lay motionless.

Silence.

Pulling his dagger free, Grom began the climb down from atop its skull. He used one of the curling horns as a foothold, allowing himself to slip down further.

Svern watched with morbid fascination as his father used the dragon's lip and exposed gums to plant his feet before hopping down. He landed with a *thud*, shaking the dust that'd coated his cloak.

Grom approached Svern slowly, moving with a slight limp. From the corner of his eye, Svern spied Allos making his way to them.

Placing one hand on Svern's shoulder, Grom held the bloody dagger out to him with the other and grinned. "The day is not over," his father said. "There is much work to be done." Moving the hand from his shoulder, Grom smeared blood across Svern's forehead.

"You killed it?" Allos asked Grom, his attention fixed on the dragon's behemoth corpse. Already, flies were swarming around its gaping wounds, nostrils, and open mouth.

Eyes full of pride gleamed back into Svern's, pride from a warrior, a legend, a father... *his* father.

Taking the dagger, Svern faced Allos. "*We* killed it. And you? You have graves to dig."

Allos shrugged. "Only fair, I s'pose."

Seeing his father produce a skinning knife, Svern took it as the sign to begin the days of work that lay ahead of them. Together, father and son walked toward the dragon, their kill, their trophy, to their new lives.

LAST SUPPER

JOYCE BEVC

LIBBY STROLLS past the fresh meat on display in Food World. *Wide selection. I wonder where they bought their grinder.* The butcher standing behind the counter smiles. "Can I help you?"

"Nothing right now. Thanks. But where do you keep the spices for flavoring meat?"

"Aisle 3."

Libby pushes her shopping cart past the ready-to-go pie crust and stops. *Interesting idea but I would need to find a recipe first. Might be too much prep work.*

Libby's cart full of aluminum foil and plastic wrap won't raise suspicion. This month is hunting season. For all anyone knows, Libby bagged a ten-point buck. *Thank God the pandemic made buying a big freezer the norm.*

Like most changes, it started small. Libby's foray into traditional keto was short-lived. Her weight loss was minimal but her appetite for meat was awakened. Being a lifelong carnivore should have clued Libby into her special need, but meat is typically served in a bastardized form with other food. Meatloaf barely deserves the title 'meat'. Breadcrumbs, onions, who-knows-what-else masks the glorious purity of the animal flesh itself.

The best cuts are gustatory heaven but even the gristly and fatty portions offer a delight no pastry, tiramisu, or cheesecake could begin to match.

Libby stands mesmerized by the choices in the seasoning aisle. An index card display designed to school shoppers on the benefits of dry rubs, wet rubs, garlic, curry, and thyme whet her appetite. Maybe someday, if her appetite ever falters, seasoning will matter. For now, nothing satisfies like the pure unadulterated taste of meat.

———

Libby doesn't have a finished basement. Words are funny. It would be inaccurate to say the basement was finished yet often finishing occurred in the basement. The first time was two years ago. Her match from Stumble-Into-Love was a disappointment.

Harry had presumptuously pranced through the house in an inappropriate posture of ownership. He had such unwarranted self-esteem. Harry expected to have his way. He expected to call the shots but lacked the foresight to anticipate the shot Libby put through his heart. Libby's behavior shocked her at the time but not because of the moral implications. Whether the shooting was self-defense or murder was moot because it created a mess to clean up and Libby hated housework.

Disposing of that first body was a learning experience. Instinctively, and from years of watching crime shows, Libby knew she could not allow Harry's body to decompose and smell. That covid-inspired chest freezer in the basement would come in handy. To protect her true identity in the morass of online dating, Libby used a burner phone and fake name. She didn't fear detection but what should be done with the meat formerly known as Harry . . .

Hacksaw. De-bone. Cut meat into individual serving portions and freeze. Cannibalism was a means to dispose of the body. Her taste for human flesh over beef or pork had not yet fully blossomed. Initially, preserving Harry's meat was done to conceal evidence of his demise.

The first package of Harry thawed a week later on the kitchen counter. The thought of devouring another human being as food did not disgust Libby. Only a curiosity about the taste accounted for the hesitancy in Libby's first nibble. That initial bite was followed by mouthfuls of medium rare Harry. Absolutely delicious.

Although Harry deserved his fate, Libby struggled to justify her next gourmet feast. . . until the hunger grew too massive to resist. *Impossible meats will never replace the mammalian drive to subsist on the flesh of other creatures. If it is legal and acceptable to consume cows, pigs, and chickens, then why not humans?* Surely cannibalism is justified as an inherent part of the argument that one's survival permits killing.

Libby hunts her prey on Stumble-Into-Love. To elude apprehension, she creates a new profile along with a new email address and burner phone number each time she tracks a quarry. Libby becomes adept at identifying male profiles with seemingly fake information, then immediately communicates offline to leave minimal contact trails. Libby snickers when people say online dating is frustrating. For her, it is immensely satisfying, so much so that she gained thirty pounds in her first year of hunting online.

Libby finishes the preparation and preservation of Jonathan, filling her freezer. She leaves an eight-ounce filet for tonight's dinner. *It is interesting how no two humans taste the same. I cannot tell the difference between organic chicken and regular, but I can tell Harry was a carnivore and Jonathan a vegan from how they taste.*

Libby pours herself a big glass of cabernet and places the plate of sizzling steak on her finest linen tablecloth. Fresh meat deserves fine china and lace. Side dishes only serve to distract from the magnificence of the entree. If meat is your primary joy, why sully your palate with potatoes or salad?

Jonathan gives Libby immense pleasure. She savors the taste of him. Young veal-like meat has become her favorite. Her searches on Stumble-Into-Love make her feel like a cougar in the quest for young flesh but a jury of her peers would understand and forgive.

Libby lets the feel of the warm, red meat linger in her mouth. She chews slowly, deliberately, and wants the taste to last forever. Swallowing is bittersweet because the flavor leaves her mouth but as long as more Jonathan lies on her plate, another opportunity for gustatory frenzy awaits. Libby spends a good twenty minutes enjoying her supper. The last bite goes down with the sadness the finality of any wonderful experience brings.

After dinner, Libby changes into her purging clothing. . . sweatpants and a torn, pink Mr. Bubble t-shirt from the thrift store. She kneels next to the commode and presses her finger behind her tongue. In a matter of minutes, Jonathan is purged. Each upchuck carries with it a nanosecond of panic that the meat will somehow make its way into Libby's windpipe and choke her. A fitting punishment that worries Libby during her fleeting moments of guilt. *If only I could meet someone named Chuck, the irony would be sublime.*

Anyone watching Libby might consider this disgusting, but her weight would balloon if she consumed this much meat without purging. The purging aspect of Libby's gluttony repulses her, but by now it has become routine. A person can get used to just about anything, even daily regurgitation.

Libby wipes the slimy mucus hanging from her lower lip and flushes the toilet for the sixth time. She walks gingerly to the refrigerator and takes a swig of buttermilk from its plastic container. Stomach acid wreaks havoc on the esophageal lining, so Libby follows each session with a soothing chaser.

After a warm shower, Libby changes into her PJ's and burrows herself under the covers of her king-size bed. A TLC TV network program about international love mismatches plays while Libby fires up her Chromebook and logs onto Stumble-Into-Love. Brandon under 'New Members' catches her eye. Red flags abound.

Professional male, well-traveled, enjoys nights in front of the fireplace. Libby chuckles to herself. *How about nights having your thigh meat cooking over my open fire?* Libby studies the rest of his profile. Libby shoots out her tried-and-true introductory message to Brandon. In a matter of minutes, she receives his reply and directs him to call her newest burner phone number.

———

Normally Libby harvests her match's meat on the first date, but since her freezer was full of Jonathan, she had to bide her time reeling in Brandon. "Come over to my place. Let's just Netflix and chill," Libby suggested each time they planned to get together during those three weeks. Brandon did not realize Libby could not risk being seen in public with him.

"Let me take you out for a steak dinner tomorrow," Brandon practically begged. "You said you loved meat."

Libby smiled. "I don't want to share you with the world. I just want you all to myself right here in front of the fireplace."

Brandon tenderly kissed Libby. *Oh my God! This is crazy-*

town! Kissing my food while it is still alive! It's taking everything in me not to bite off his lip and have myself some Brandon tartare.

"Believe me, I'm not complaining," Brandon was earnest. "I'm happy we're getting to know each other so well one-on-one."

"I'll make a steak dinner for you here tomorrow night," Libby promised.

———

All day long Libby debated serving Jonathan to Brandon. The flavor would be unique, but Libby could blame it on an old family marinade recipe. Mention an obscure seasoning most people have never tasted, and Brandon would be none the wiser.

Her decision made, Libby set the last two Jonathan filets on the kitchen counter to thaw. After weeks of Netflix with Brandon, the basement freezer was empty. Tonight would be the night. A romantic last supper with Brandon and then time to restock the stash of meat. Libby is overcome with sadness as she plans the evening meal. Brandon was the nicest man she ever dated. He was kind, genuinely liked her, and even hinted at growing feelings of love. It was too bad she needed more meat.

When Libby hears knocking and answers the door, Brandon stands holding a bottle of red wine and a bouquet of flowers. He gives Libby a quick kiss as he enters. "Something smells good!"

Libby gulps. The kiss stirs her appetite. She places the flowers in a vase on the dining room table. For this special occasion, the fine linen tablecloth lies under place settings for two. For the first time ever, Libby is prepared to share her spoils.

Libby realizes, to her amazement, that she is in love.

Spending time with the not-yet-slaughtered Brandon has awakened feelings new to her. Deep affection. Respect. *Brandon is the kind of man I want to be with. He is the best thing that ever happened to me. He makes me a better person.*

Libby sits at the table while Brandon pours wine into their glasses. Scalloped potatoes and brussels sprouts accompany the filets on each of their dishes. For this special occasion, Libby wants everything to be perfect. Brandon expects side dishes so he will get them.

"Everything looks great," Brandon smiles.

"Thank you. Dig in."

Brandon cuts into his steak and takes his first taste of Jonathan. Libby studies him as he chews. Brandon appears thoughtful, not alarmed, as an expression of curiosity and intrigue crosses his face.

"What kind of meat is this? It doesn't taste like beef."

"You have a sophisticated palate. It's not beef. Do you like it?"

"I've never tasted anything like this before."

"The meat is wild game. I ordered it online. It has a unique flavor and I soaked it in a special marinade."

Brandon smiles and continues to consume Jonathan's flesh.

Conversation falters as the pleasure of food takes precedence. Libby's heart soars with love as Brandon cleans his plate. People work hard all their lives, hoping at some point they will be free to do as they please. *Everyone can do whatever they want every moment.*

———

Libby smooths the wrinkles from her lace tablecloth and sets the table for herself. Her mouth waters with anticipation.

Today is a fresh meat day. The first time Libby will consume Brandon's flesh.

Cliches about love are all wrong. It does not fade over time. It deepens. It grows until it overwhelms all else. Libby had fallen for Brandon completely, and he for her.

Libby takes the first bite of Brandon. As expected, he cooked up to be her most delicious meal ever. Libby had become unable to bear time apart from Brandon. Now they would be united forever. Libby would devour Brandon and not purge. He would thus truly become part of her. Libby's love for Brandon is infinite.

———

Joyce has been writing short stories, novels and stage plays in a variety of genres. She's been published in Strangest Fiction Volume 2 and the Mensa Bulletin.

HEROES' GARDEN

SADIE LEEWOOD

THE SCENT of roasted lamb greeted Sir Roddnee as he entered the clearing. The bright sunlight illuminating the cottage and its abundant garden created a welcome sight after many days spent stumbling through the dim twilight of the ancient forest.

The knight was weak with hunger, having lost his steed and pack of supplies three days earlier to a steep gulley. His first official quest had not gone well so far, but finding this quaint little house, and the savory smoke rising from its tiny chimney, boded well. For the first time in three days, he didn't regret his decision to keep going.

He approached the home—a modest building built of logs and roofed with thatch. The garden surrounding it, in contrast, provided an audacious display of color and size. Flowering pea vines climbed trellises higher than the roof. The lower-growing flowers ranged in color from blood red to the palest blue-violet. Posts with ropes tied to them tamed the greenery into neat rectangular patches, making the dirt paths between the lush growth walkable.

"Hallo! Is anyone home?" he bellowed. He was surprised by the scratchy timbre of his dry throat.

A small part of him feared this was a hallucination, but he could feel the stones of the path to the house under his boots, and smell the fragrant breeze wafting from the closest garden patch: lavender and rosemary.

A carrot's thick top stuck up from the ground under a starburst of hairy green leaves. He looked to the house for a sign of life. His hunger dared him to grab it and eat it raw.

A silvery head with wide eyes appeared in a round window, then disappeared. Roddnee, relieved, abandoned his thieving and walked closer to the house.

"I am a knight of West Umberland, traveling on the orders of the king. I ask that you share your meal so that I may continue my quest."

The door's creaking heralded the occupant's emergence. She was small–shorter than the knob centered on the door. Her hair, in a simple braid, shone to rival the king's finest silver flatware.

The knight bowed. "Good afternoon, m'lady. I am Sir Roddnee Mintel of West Umberland, sent by order–"

"I heard you, it's fine. Please join me." The tiny woman, whose age could have been anywhere between thirty and seventy, smiled and nodded, waving him in. As she turned, her blue dress twirled.

After a quiet, filling meal of greasy, spiced lamb, minted jelly, and boiled turnips, Roddnee found himself once again in possession of his manners. "Oh, my dear lady, I apologize. I have been lost in the woods for days, surviving on berries and leaves. I will find a way to repay you for this life-saving feast!"

Sitting across the small wooden table, her plate empty, the woman smiled warmly. "Think nothing of it, Sir Knight. I am honored to provide you with sustenance for your quest." She stood and took away his plate of bone and gristle, then turned back. "Although…perhaps you would tell me about your quest? I don't get much in the way of entertainment here."

Roddnee held a hand over his mouth to suppress a hearty burp. "Of course, m'lady. I am sure you are familiar with the destruction wreaked by the dragon that dwells in the mountain caves above your home?"

She put a kettle onto the hook in the fireplace. "Of course. I see the beast often. It flies overhead on its way to the city and farms, scaring me half to death!"

His plate mail clanked as he sat up straighter on his stool. It was uncomfortable, but if he had not been wearing it at all times, it would have been lost to the gulley along with his horse. "The king called for knights willing to risk life and limb to kill the monster. I am here to take its life and bring back its head." He tapped the pommel of his sword as if it were a foregone conclusion. Then, he remembered how uncouth it was to have a sword at the table. He hastily removed it and leaned it against the nearby wall, next to his helmet.

As she prepared herbs in a ceramic teapot, she asked, "Is there a reward for the dragon's head?"

Roddnee nodded. "Indeed, there is. Land and a title. A rare opportunity for a man to become a gentleman."

"That is an impressive boon. I can see why so many young men have come by lately."

"Many? How many?"

She walked past the table to look out the window nearest to Roddnee. "Seven. No, eight. That thin one hides behind the hollyhocks."

He looked out the window, eyes searching for what she was counting.

"Swords," she explained, walking back to the fireplace. "When the men come down the mountain, running and screaming, they shed their swords and weapons. They seem to think that will stop its pursuit."

He looked out again and found them. Sticking straight up out of the ground like tall metal crosses. They were used in place of wooden posts in some of the garden beds. Suddenly his lamb sat uneasily in his stomach.

"Pursuit?"

"The dragon follows them. But how can you outrun a flying demon like that? Once the battle begins, it will be finished, one way or another. Tea?" She toddled over awkwardly with a large tray laden with cups, saucers, and a steaming teapot.

His heartbeat now pounding quickly, the knight nodded, happy for the distraction. She poured the tea into a normal-sized cup for the knight, and a half-sized one for herself.

As he sipped the sweet, herby liquid, the knight asked, "So what is your story, good lady? This is quite a ways from even the furthest farms of the realm."

Taking her seat with a small hop, she smiled knowingly. "Sir Knight, unlike some, I do not thrive in the hustle and bustle of the city, nor do I wish to be a servant of the crown." She narrowed her eyes and looked at him sideways, "Please don't you go telling the king about that last part!"

He chuckled.

"You must see that at my size, society is not built for me. I keep to myself–except for the occasional visitor–and tend my garden. I trade for goods with the traveling trade folk, so I never want for anything for very long. Even gossip." She took a small sip, then put down her cup abruptly and sat up straight. "I have a confession to make. I have deceived you."

Roddnee choked on his tea.

The lady smiled. "I already knew about the king's call for knights. I heard about it months back from a poet. He bartered some honey and cabbages for a poem about my heroes' garden. I just enjoyed hearing about it again from you. I apologize."

"No harm done, m'lady. I cannot fault you for enjoying some conversation." He emptied his cup. When he placed it down, she filled it again. "This herb mix is quite new to me. I can taste something spicy in there--"

"Isn't it a nice, bright flavor? Would you believe it's not an herb at all? Well, not directly." She got up and went to a countertop of jars of all colors and sizes and selected one, bringing it over to the knight. The goo inside was a pinkish color and the paper label read: "Firebreath Honey".

He feigned fright. "Firebreath? Will I soon be belching flame?"

"Hah! That would surely give you an advantage against the dragon, wouldn't it?" She shook her head, walking the jar back to its home. "No, the name comes from a fiery red flower that blooms at the end of summer. When the bees discover it, they will have no other flower until it all dies away. The honey is a beautiful pink at that time, and the spicy flavor is imbued therein. Quite a delicacy, I think, as travelers always want more when they return."

As she sat down opposite him again, the knight held his hands tightly around the mug, enjoying its warmth, and looked around the cottage. Soot had stained the hearth, but the rest of the space was bright and colorful. Plants in pots as well as drying herbs hung from rafters. A myriad of jars were stacked on every shelf and surface–including a pile of books. A ladder with rungs twice as frequent as a man's step led up to a small loft of pale yellow bedding.

"Your home is delightful, miss…" He had forgotten his manners yet again. "I beg your pardon, but I have not asked for your name. My time in the woods left me quite uncivilized."

She laughed lightly. "I was wondering if you'd ever ask. I

am Octavia Nurmroot." She stood and curtsied, pulling her well-worn apron out to the sides. "A pleasure to make your acquaintance, Sir Roddnee Mintel of West Umberland."

"Well, Madam Nurmroot, the pleasure is all mine. And I mean it, your home is exquisitely cozy and pleasant. I was born to be a farmer, you see. Your home reminds me of my own before the pestilence took that all away. Of all the places I might have wandered, I am very lucky to have come across your hospitality before I made for the mountain."

She blushed and looked into her cup for a moment. "Sir Roddnee, do you truly mean to fight and kill the dragon? To drag its head back to the king?"

"I do."

"Even knowing how many men, young and strong like yourself, have fled in terror, only to be consumed?"

He straightened up, feeling warm. "I do."

She nodded, slowly filling his teacup once more. "I am sorry to hear that. I do wish you'd reconsider. I could send you back to the city with rare treats and herbs you could sell and–"

Goosebumps sprung up along his arms, yet the room felt very hot. "I must ask you to refrain from your pleading. I have taken on this quest and I will see the vile creature dispatched."

"I understand."

In silence, they sipped tea.

Roddnee tried to blame the strange feelings overcoming him on eating so much after nearly starving. He felt lightheaded in a way that reminded him of late nights at the pub when he was still just a farmer's son. The cottage was stifling, and sweat soaked his blond curls.

Octavia seemed to notice his discomfort. "How about a walk around the garden? It is a nice, cool day, and the bees are fascinating to watch."

Stumbling to his feet, Roddnee reached for his sword.

"Oh, you won't need that out there," she tutted as she opened the door.

Despite being trained to never go unarmed or unprotected, he obeyed and followed, empty-handed.

When they walked outside, she reached into her apron pocket and pulled out a small bell. She shook it, though Roddnee heard nothing, and then she placed it back in her pocket.

He looked at her, raising an eyebrow.

"For the bees, Sir Knight. It lets them know I'm not a threat. Come this way."

She led Roddnee, who now had trouble keeping his feet under him, down a path of beaten earth that curved into a grove of trees and opened into a clearing. He didn't see any hives.

"Where are the bees?"

"In the next clearing. But they will not like the clang of that armor. You'll be stung a thousand times. Could you kindly take it off and leave it here? It will only be for a few minutes."

It made perfect sense to Roddnee, and he was incredibly hot. Taking the armor off would be a blessed relief. He took his time, given the balance issues he was experiencing. He let each piece clatter to the ground, enjoying the cool breeze that followed its removal. When he wore only his chainmail and undergarments, he walked towards Octavia.

"Oh, dear. That chainmail will have to go as well. So noisy!"

Of course. He did not want to scare the bees. Nodding numbly, he pulled the chainmail shirt off over his head. It puddled to the ground with a tinkling sound.

He stepped to meet her in the center of the clearing.

"On to see beeeeezz?" he slurred.

"I'm afraid I have another creature to show you, Sir Knight. I have deceived you yet again."

A shadow passed overhead, and a strong wind blew. Roddnee, confused and tired, sat down hard and looked up. A black and gold dragon, its wingspan the length of ten horses laid end-to-end, descended into the clearing. It landed with a jarring thump that upset Roddnee's aching head.

Octavia stood as tall as she could, her eyes fiery. If Roddnee could still feel fear, he would have been as intimidated by her as the dragon. "I cannot let you harm my gorgeous baby. I raised Goldie from an egg after some cruel knights slew her mother on the mountain. She is my only companion in this world and deserves to live."

Octavia reached up and stroked the dragon's neck, which now curled around her. "She protects me and brings me meat. You had some of that lamb earlier. And I protect her and bring her meat."

Roddnee nodded, but his mind had fogged far beyond understanding. He watched with clouded eyes as the tiny woman pointed at him. The dragon's mouth opened and fire barrelled toward him.

–

Close to dusk, Goldie dozed peacefully, feeling the effects of the tea the knight had enjoyed. The firebreath honey, while pleasantly intoxicating to humans, was a powerful soporific for dragons. A scorch mark was all that remained of Sir Roddnee Mintel.

Octavia returned to the clearing. She had buried the knight's armor deep in the woods, well past the bee hives. His sword now stood sentinel over a bed of fava beans. She carried a lantern, a stick, a bucket, and a scrubbing brush.

She invited most young men intent on dragon slaying to see the bees, but it was only when Goldie's breath became unbearable that Octavia needed to use a knight to serve her dragon a dose of sedative. Hiding the drug in her food was the only way to get her to take her medicine.

Hiking up her skirt, Octavia climbed onto a forepaw and used the stick to keep Goldie's upper lip out of the way. She dipped her brush into the bucket of minty liquid and scrubbed the dragon's needle-like teeth, each almost half her height. She could get them all cleaned in one night with this induced sleep, and she wouldn't need to do another scrub for at least a season.

More than two hours later, exhausted and sweaty, Octavia returned to her cottage. She climbed her ladder and hung her lantern over her bed. The poem she had commissioned a few months before lay beside her pillow. She enjoyed reading it before going to sleep, in her cozy little cottage at the foot of the mountain.

Steel crosses honour not the noblemen
Whose speed betrayed them so well
But those who would turn back to their homeland
And leave the mountain to whom therein dwell

KILL THE SADNESS

SADIE LEEWOOD

ROBERT DIDN'T KNOW she was watching.

He walked away from his family's campsite along the path toward the latrines. The evening's dew from the short grass seeped into his flannel pajama bottoms. A silent Milky Way loomed across the blue-black sky. Crickets practiced their never-finished symphony.

Dot, who had trained to be silent in almost any situation, felt like her heartbeat echoed throughout the meadow. Missions were usually easy. This passion project of hers ignited all kinds of feelings – joy, wonder, seething anger – by which normal missions were never affected. She adjusted the focus on her night-vision goggles nervously and squinted as a swing of his flashlight beam burst across her eyes like a green flame.

From her vantage point, twelve feet up a broadleaf tree and fifty feet from the meadow, she watched him turn off the path into the taller grass. He put his flashlight into his mouth and reached for his waist. His back faced her, but she assumed he was relieving himself there rather than trekking to the latrines.

The flashlight flickered out. The plastic handle muffled his curse as he adjusted himself. Before he could grab the light, it flickered back on, then off again.

The meadow lit up like daylight as thousands of fireflies responded to his accidental 'hello'.

Looking away after the flash blinded her through the goggles, Dot reached into her vest's pocket and pulled out a Viper XS, a small dart gun.

Robert stayed where he was, unmoving, for almost a full minute. Then he took the flashlight out of his mouth and slapped its base. It blinked on, then off. Another array of electric green pinpoints appeared and then disappeared. This was the moment she had aimed for. She would witness his moment of inspiration. And then end his life.

———

Her supervisor, Benedict, had asked her into his office to assign her the mission. "An A3. Should be no contact, and no opposing force," he said as he handed her the file folder.

A Level 3 Adjustment. Level 3 was keeping someone from dying. No opposing force was unusual. Usually, you had to fight a rogue time traveler to keep your target alive.

"This is not a Correction." He lowered his voice, glancing out the office window at the cubicles. "This is a favor. Head of HR. His wife's father died in a car accident on a work trip when she was just a kid."

Dot opened the folder, scanning the top sheet. She'd never done an unofficial mission before. She wasn't sure she wanted to.

In her years of making Corrections to the timeline, she had plenty of time to ponder the ethics of the work. Fixing what criminal travelers had broken was one thing. But bringing someone back who had died in a natural way? So many people would love to have their tragedies undone, but this one jerk gets resurrected because of a work connection? How many ripples would that cause? Was he even a good person?

Worst of all, only Dot would remember the mission. Everyone else would have lived in the corrected timeline. The favoritism would go unpunished.

She was about to close the folder and decline the mission when she noticed the date on the dossier. April 17, 1994. The location was also close to ideal: upstate New York.

Clutching the folder tightly, she stood up and nodded to her supervisor. "Thanks, boss. I'll take care of it."

Her chance had finally come. The date and location were too perfect to pass up. She could easily camp out for a few months after completing her assignment, make her way South to the Pocono Mountains, and find Robert Allen Pritchard himself. What she was about to do was illegal, and went against everything the Corrections Agency stood for, but it was the only way she knew to save her friend.

———

The official mission was a cakewalk. In a rented cabin in the middle of nowhere, the subject had no way of communicating with the outside world except by landline. A cable snipped, a fuse removed, and Mr. Specialpants was trapped in his posh cabin with his lady friend – presumably she was the subject of his "work".

Dot watched all day from behind a bush along the tree line. The subject – who appeared intoxicated to the point of stumbling – tried to get the car to start a few times. When that proved fruitless, he mostly just yelled pathetically at the trees or his companion. In the early evening, he flagged down the mailman. The mail carrier refused to give him a ride but promised to pass on a message. When midnight struck, the mission was complete.

Then came Dot's project.

The protocol for living for any extended period in the past was very stringent.

- Remain low or no contact with other people.
- Only eat to survive.
- Avoid surveillance by people and technology.
- All interactions are potential ripples.

One example scenario from her training always stuck with Dot: a Corrections Agent gets injured. He, of course, cannot go to a hospital, so instead he finds a drugstore and buys supplies to treat himself. He's fine and can complete his mission and return to the present. However, among the supplies he bought from the store was the last package of sterile gauze on the shelves. A mother shopping later that day doesn't buy gauze because the store now needs to order more. Then, her son is injured at home and they use regular cloth to dress his wound. He develops an infection and later dies. That boy would have been the future father of a scientist who would have developed cold fusion in the early 2000s.

Only one agent remembered that timeline, so was it true? Either way, it was a great story to scare rookie Corrections Agents.

Dot planned to make her way to the Poconos on foot. It would take a while, but walking would pass the time. She had packed some unauthorized supplies before coming to 1994: a lightweight tent, an inflatable bedroll, and powdered nourishment. Staying to the deep forests and foothills, she managed to almost completely avoid other people and still made it to Cranberry Run Campground with a month to spare.

Another item she brought with her was a small tablet loaded with e-books and movies. Media content of any kind was off-limits on missions, a provision known as the Tannen Protocol. The tablet contained the entire six-book series of *The Fae Academy Chronicles*, all seven movies, and an assortment of guides and graphic novels.

On the edge of the campground, she pitched her tent and laid in for weeks of waiting, reading, and watching.

———

Dot was twelve when the first Fae Academy book, *The First Year Jitters* was published. It followed the adventures of Binkelle Strum, the elite school's first half-goblin student, as she tried to fit in with the many diverse creatures attending the Fae Academy. And "jitters" were more than just nerves. They were a species of their own: a small, spiky pest that latched onto people who lacked confidence. Binkelle and her newly-made friends helped to rid the whole school of the jitters and became heroes.

She probably read the first book twenty times before the second one came out. It was her *everything* in that hellish year of middle school when her few friends seemed to transform into nasty, lipstick-wearing she-beasts overnight. Suddenly they were too mature for make-believe, while Dot could have kept playing pretend in homemade costumes forever. It didn't help that her small elementary school fed into a much larger middle school, or that she was biracial in a mostly mono-chrome population.

The Fae Academy series made middle school and high school bearable. Bink was her inspiration, embracing both her halfling and goblin heritages. Dot could always escape her reality and live in Bink's instead. It was during lunch in her sophomore year, reading book four, *The Trek to Asher's Hollow*, that she finally made a true friend. Sophie, with her baggy boy clothes and green Manic Panic'ed hair, had walked up, brought out her own tattered hardback copy, and asked if she could sit with Dot. They were inseparable after that, weirdos with a common cause. Later that year, they dressed up – Dot as Binkelle, Sophie as Greenus the Wood Faerie – for a midnight release of book five: *The Moon's Lost Children*.

Dot brought the books to college, and then to her first apartment. She reread them often. She went to the movie openings. She bought the DVDs. They were her escape whenever the world was too much for her. She had a throw blanket that sported the crest of the Fae Academy. She bought prints of character fanart for her walls. She named her cat "Tvass" after Bink's familiar, a lizard who wore a mushroom hat. Calling her a superfan would have been an understatement. Dot's life ever since she read that first book had been forged in the halls of The Fae Academy.

So, when a headline popped into her feed that read "YA Author Under Investigation for Inappropriate Relationship with Minor", the light in Dot's life began to dim. Several girls and women came forth. Some were as young as fourteen when he invited them to his home. He was arrested, tried, and eventually imprisoned. The man who had underwritten the plot of Dot's life was a pedophile. A truly disgusting and prolific one.

Some Fae Academy fans just moved on, accepting that the work could be enjoyed even if the creator was a monster. They could separate the source from the art. Dot could not.

Other former fans divorced themselves from the Fae Academy entirely. They destroyed their books, threw out their Fae-branded belongings, and covered up their Fae-inspired tattoos. Dot had trouble with this, too. The Academy was a huge part of her life – of who she was. How could she just pretend it never existed?

If Dot's light had dimmed, her friend and roommate Sophie's had been all but snuffed out. Dot watched as her friend spent the better part of two years in a walking depression. Sophie drank a lot, didn't eat right, and just went through the motions of life. Her room in their apartment became a trash heap. Dot had to venture in there to find missing dishes and cups weekly to wash them or they would have run out.

When Sophie's inability to get out of bed regularly got her fired, she finally listened to Dot and sought professional help. After many sessions, her therapist convinced her that she was essentially in mourning. And, like when a person we love dies, the beautiful things the books had imbued in her would remain. She needed to move on. The best way to do that was to leave the Fae Academy behind her, selling all the books, movies, and paraphernalia she could, and throwing away the rest. In solidarity, Dot also sold her Fae Academy collection.

It took months to rid themselves of everything. There were plenty of people still willing to enjoy the Fae Academy, so they made a healthy sum from selling their merchandise. That was good, because they had to buy new pictures for the walls, new mugs, and a new shower curtain to replace the Fae Academy merchandise. They let Tvass keep his name. "He just *looks* like a Tvass, you know?" Sophie said.

One book they couldn't find a buyer for was "The Magnificent World of The Fae Academy" kids book – one of those pseudo books that are mostly photos from the movies. As Dot carried it and a few other last books to the garbage, it slipped from the pile and fell, opening to the author interview page as if guided by an unseen hand:

What was the inspiration for the Fae Academy books?

"I've always been fascinated by the idea of other worlds, perhaps overlapping with ours. But I think the real lightning bolt moment was when I was in college, and I was camping with my parents in the Poconos. I was feeling silly camping with them, sharing a tent, thinking I was this big adult now. I was too old for campfires and hot dogs and ghost stories.

"The forest sounds kept waking me up, so I went walking in the middle of the night to see the stars. And then my flashlight blinked out – then back on – then off again. And then all the lightning bugs blinked at me. A whole mass of them, a whole meadow of them. It was amazing. Like a world of the tiny and unseen *shouting* at me to believe.

"And after that, I did believe. And the characters and the stories just kind of wrote themselves."

Dot knelt on the floor, reading and rereading the passage. Sophie walked in, grabbing another box destined for the dumpster. "What are you doing?"

Dot looked up at her pale, skinny friend, and smiled. "I know what I'm going to do now. I'm going to fix everything."

———

The Viper XS held a 2-part formula that, once combined, would form the slow-working neurotoxin she would use to kill Robert Pritchard. Another smuggled item. She slid her finger into the side tube, pushing the button to start the mixing process.

In the meadow, Robert flashed his light again. He walked further into the grass and sat down, carefully catching a few fireflies in his hand before letting them take off again.

During the lonely weeks of reading and watching all the Fae Academy media, her anger had softened. She had avoided the stories for six years now, and she was thrilled to be back in the hallowed halls, hanging with Bink's crew on the mezzanine as they planned the confidence ambush that would trap the Jitters in a crossfire of encouraging phrases between friends. The movies, with their iconic music and child actors who got their big breaks in the films, brought back so many joyful memories. She and Sophie had watched the movies every year over holiday breaks. Their Christmas tree was topped with a light-up Firefly Flask instead of a star, just like in the books. Both had agreed that creatures existing in a world without Christianity wouldn't celebrate Christmas, but that logic didn't matter because the stories were so fun.

The chemical solution was ready. She held the gun up, catching Robert's center of mass in the sight. Her heart was still beating too fast, and her finger quivered.

One shot would destroy all that pain and devastation. It would stop all that abuse.

But it would also remove a whole universe from the world.

She was going to kill Binkelle and Greenus and The Academy. Worst of all, she might never be friends with Sophie, at least not in the same way. She lowered the gun.

Was this the only way to solve the problem? Was there a better way? Should she catch him at some other time, after he started writing? Could she allow him to create the stories but still make sure he didn't end up as that monster?

Robert swept his arm up, catching another bug. He laughed as he smashed his hands together, leaving a fluorescent streak of firefly guts across his palm.

Dot lifted the gun, aimed, and shot in a single motion.

Robert slapped a glowing hand over his shoulder, to squash what he thought was a mosquito. He stood, his reverie ended, and walked back toward his tent.

"For Sophie," she whispered.

———

After a night strapped to her tree branch, Dot was awakened by frantic screams from Robert's tent as his parents found him cold and unresponsive. She watched the father, in flip-flops and boxer shorts, run down the trail that led to the ranger station.

Hearing only soft sobs from the tent, Dot took the opportunity to extract herself from the tree and make her way carefully back to her camp. She walked slowly, working out the cricks in her neck and legs. Her personal mission was accomplished. But instead of relief, she felt numb and tired.

As she packed her things, the tablet and dart gun popped and cracked in the firepit. She couldn't show up at headquarters with anything but what the mission required.

This had never been about reaching some better solution, she reminded herself. This was about mitigating pain. And unfortunately, given how time travel worked, that pain would still be there for her. She alone would remember. But everyone else would be free.

After scattering the ashes of her contraband in a swift little brook, she found a secluded clearing in the woods and turned the knob on her portable "door", as they called it at the Agency. It was a white, handheld sphere with a smooth carrying handle. A yellow-white crackling orb grew from the device and enveloped Dot.

———

The return to the present was ordinary. Like always, no one remembered her official mission, let alone her secret one. She just appeared in the transit room in a changed world.

In the debrief, she repeated the phony mission details outlined in the dossier Benedict had provided. She was instructed to say that the man in the cabin needed to be saved to ensure the timeline was safe. Management was surprised by her report, because the person she saved from driving drunk in 1994 had gone on to die in a booze-induced wreck three years later along with his eight-year-old daughter. Dot tried to keep her face neutral. The Head of HR's wife was now long dead because of her own request to save her father, and only Dot knew.

"I followed the dossier to the letter," she insisted. Management agreed she had done nothing wrong. Correcting the timeline doesn't always work out as expected.

Dot went home to find a stranger sharing her apartment. She was not roommates with Sophie in this new timeline. Through Facebook, she found that Sophie lived a few states away, in Maryland. Dot used some vacation time for a road trip.

In a supermarket in a suburb of Baltimore, Dot, carrying a basket of hastily grabbed food items, approached Sophie. She looked very different from what Dot remembered. Dot was thrilled to see she was a healthy weight – even a little plump, and her hair was an electric ombre of orange and yellow that resembled an upside-down poppy. A small child with curly hair was sitting in the seat of her cart.

"Sophie? Is that you?"

Sophie looked at Dot blankly.

"Dot? From high school? We used to sit at the same table at lunch sometimes?"

"Oh my gosh, Dot! Wow! It's been so long!"

In a few minutes of awkward conversation, Dot learned that Sophie was helping her sister by babysitting her niece and running errands, that she was a successful graphic designer, and that she still loved to read. Dot said goodbye when the toddler started squirming, left her shopping basket on a shelf, and went to her car to cry.

Robert Allen Pritchard was not a famous author in this new world, and the Fae Academy never existed. Her friend was happy again, but no longer her friend. Was this the cost of her crime?

She reviewed the archives of the Corrections Agency to try

to find any significant ripples caused by Pritchard's death. It's not easy to find evidence of a negative, but she concluded that the timeline endured just fine without the pedophile author's presence. Sure, the actors she knew as Binkelle and Greenus had started their careers at a slower pace, but found themselves in the same big roles in Disney and Superhero films anyway. In Dot's own home, a framed watercolor print that had originally depicted the Fae Academy and its surrounding magical valley now showed an enormous colony tree surrounded by the majestic flying creatures from Martha Wells' Raksura books. The artist was the same – only the subject matter had changed.

A dozen girls did not have their childhood stolen by Pritchard. Thousands of Fae Academy fans did not have their hearts broken. And Sophie was going to be OK. Dot had to accept that it was worth it. She had considered this possible outcome before she left for 1994. It was just so much harder to live with than she had anticipated.

Even work had become different. Corrections Agency training had led her to believe rogue time travelers were only out for selfish or nefarious causes. After her foray into time banditry, she questioned whether the men and women she was sent to stop were just as well-meaning as her. Maybe it was always wrong to take risks with the timeline. But maybe it wasn't.

Dot could still recall the stories of the Academy. Sometimes she let the adventures play out in her mind, like a bittersweet memory. She did her best to replace those stories by reading other books. The timeline had healed itself the moment Pritchard died, but Dot would take longer to finish her own healing process.

SOUL BROTHER

SADIE LEEWOOD

STATE OF CALIFORNIA

San Mateo County   SUPERIOR COURT = CRIMINAL
Docket No. 25-SM-902421-Z

VIDEO TRANSCRIPTION
Exhibit - A

YOUTUBE VIDEO TITLED "Soul Brother Part 1" posted
by user DirkNirkem (AKA Dirk Matthew Tanner) on the
MaxRunnerz YouTube Channel on November 4, 2024.

[Video begins. Left and right positions are from the
perspective of the viewer. Dirk's face is centered, taking up
most of the vertical space of the video. Behind him, to the left,
the edge of a bed with a metal headboard can be seen. To the
right there is a desk with two monitors, a keyboard, and a
mouse. Dirk is a caucasian male, age 26, with short brown
hair and light brown eyes. He has a mole on his right cheek
below his eye. The top of a black t-shirt is visible.]

Hey! It's ya' boy, Dirk, with another video. This one, uh, is not gonna to be like my other videos. This is gonna be… something else. I'll be back soon with another speedrun video, but for now, let's get to this video. OK, so…

[sighs, looks to the left, then back at the camera]

I'm not supposed to be here.

So what do I mean by that?

I was supposed to die when I was fourteen.

[rolls eyes]

Now, I know what you're thinking. You think I did something dangerous and after almost dying I dramatically declared that [uses finger quotes] "I should have died."

No. That's not what happened.

I legit was supposed to die. I got hit by a truck. I shouldn't have survived.

Now, I'm still alive. You might ask why I'm not super happy to still be here, breathing and living and shit. "Aren't you grateful for every day, Dirk?"

[leans face closer to the camera]

Fuck no, I ain't.

[leans back to original position]

It's like…you ever stay too long at a wedding? When it's just the bride and groom's friends and some family left, and you were a second-tier guest at best, and you know none of the in-jokes and stories? You sit in the circle of folding chairs by the bar, and you laugh at the right moments, but you might as well not be there at all. You're extraneous.

[looks down]

That's my whole life–I don't belong here, on this earth. Not anymore.

The day I should have died a bunch of us were taking the trail back from tagging the abandoned train tunnels. We always painted there because we were still working on our skills and only homeless dudes ever went there so we couldn't get into trouble. That was the day I taught Telly how to do a 2-color fade.

So there's a spot where the trail crosses a four-lane road. It had a crosswalk but no lights or anything. You had to wait and watch so you didn't get squashed by a big rig. I was running ahead 'cuz I stole the hot pink paint can from Telly and she was after me.

I ran into the crosswalk without looking and I don't remember anything from then until a few days later when I woke up in the hospital. I was attached to tubes and wires and shit. My mom was sitting in a chair, sleeping, and when she heard me wake up she started crying and freaking out.

[looks down, then looks back at the camera]

I had gotten hit by an eighteen-wheeler going over fifty miles an hour. But, because I had also stolen Telly's unicorn bike helmet, my brains stayed in my head instead of painting the street a whole different shade of pink.

I was young. I recovered in just a few months, and some of my joints have metal in 'em. But seriously, something changed after that hit. Something was missing in me. I wasn't *me* anymore. I'm not even sure I'm really human anymore–not like I had been.

[leans closer to the camera]

After the accident, I couldn't tag anymore. Like, no sketching or art or anything. I loved drawing before. I was doing these stupid little comics for my friends all the time, making fun of the teachers and the asshole kids. But after–it was like I forgot how to draw completely. I would put pencil to paper and my brain just couldn't process how to make the shape I wanted anymore.

I also just stopped caring about Telly. I had the biggest crush on her before. She was my reason for being, practically, up until that truck. Holding her hand while showing her how to do something with the spray can–that was my heaven on earth. But after–she turned from this vibrant pink-and-blue light to a dull gray blob in my mind. All my friends did. Colorless copies of themselves.

And they all pulled away from me. I didn't get invited to their houses. They went to the tunnels without me. Painted over my tags like they didn't even see them. I mean, I *found* that spot. I taught half of them how to use a spray can.

[sniffles, wipes eyes]

My best friends, who were there when it happened, couldn't even nod at me when I saw them at school. They just looked right through me. Even my mom was weird to me. She would forget to make dinner for both of us. One year she forgot my birthday. It was just the two of us, so that was super shitty.

[shakes his head vigorously]

But it wasn't her. Or them. I know that. It was *me* that changed.

[looks up and to the right, frowning]

Do you know what it's like to meet amazing people online, people you have a deep connection with? I've texted with the most beautiful women and talked to them on video chats, and we can be hitting it off for weeks, but the second they want to meet in person, I know it's over.

It's the same. Every. Single. Time. They smile when they see me. They walk over to the table at the coffee shop or the bar, and they sit down.

[moves shoulders back and forth, imitating walking]

But in about three minutes they've sensed it, before their drink even shows up. They can tell I'm wrong. They get the ick. They don't know what it is. They probably think it's a sixth sense that I'm a serial killer or something. But it doesn't matter why, because they get all squirmy and frowny. They find an excuse to leave. And afterwards, they ghost me, block me, ignore me.

[throws hands up]

Now you're asking, "Why don't we feel weird about you, Dirk?" Well, friends, you're just seeing video of me. You aren't in a room with me. It's a physical thing, I think. You see my face, you look at it. But people in real life look through me, or away from me. I make them uncomfortable. There's something *fundamentally* wrong with ya' boy Dirk.

[leans forward]

Wanna know what I think happened?

I think we all have an expiration date. A date and a time when our soul goes bad, and it's no good after that. For most people it's right when they die, so it doesn't matter that it expired–they did too. All good.

But *my* time came and went. I expired twelve years ago.

I'm twenty-six now and I'm done. I've been done.

I'm always alone.

I can't keep going on like this, just pretending at being alive. That's what it feels like. Like I'm a puppet making my own body move.

[holds his palms out, shaking his hands]

And before you freak out, no, I'm not about to unalive myself. In fact, I have a plan to fix this.

[leans back in his seat]

So I started working at the new Dollar Tree back in June, and I met this guy Quinn. He's on shift with me a lot. He's like twenty-one or something. He has no family, no real friends. He lives in a group home with a buncha' other guys. They have, like, another guy that lives there that keeps them in line, like a babysitter. I think he spent some time in prison before, so he has to have someone watch him like that.

[glances to left]

He seems pretty depressed about his shitty life. Real defeatist. Does a shitty job at work, too, and it's like, the *stupidest* job, so that's really saying something. Like how do you fuck up stacking boxes on a shelf? Quinn can.

[scraping noises as he pulls his chair closer to the camera]

Anyway, so my whole theory about the expiration dates? So what if it goes the other way too? What if your expiration date is at a hundred and then you die when you're only twenty?

Ghosts! That explains ghosts!

Their soul is stuck on earth until their expiration date.

[looks off to the upper right]

Maybe that's like actually your appointment with the grim reaper. And if he takes your soul and you don't die, like me, he just goes to the next appointment and you're screwed. And if the opposite happens and you die early, you have to wait until he shows up to collect you.

[laughs]

That is a wild thought. Shit.

So anyway, my expiration date was when I was fourteen, but Quinn's is probably in his sixties or seventies. But he *hates* his life.

[raises eyebrows, staring into the camera]

He seriously one night told me that if he didn't come in the next day, that he had written in his will I could have his original vintage NES and all his games he's collected. If his roommates didn't steal them first, of course.

Like he was seriously considering offing himself. So I think it's doing him a solid taking care of it for him, right?

And I think if I kill him, then his soul–which isn't expired yet–will need someplace to go.

[points both thumbs at his chest]

Since I'm missing a soul, it should jump right in.

Makes sense, right? Like physics, like a vacuum. I have this emptiness, and his soul will fill it.

So, anyways, I offered to take Quinn out tonight for drinks

and I roofied his beer. The man is heavy, let me tell ya'. Was falling over even before I got him to the car. He's still sleeping, as you can see.

[reaches a hand out to the camera, turning the camera to the left, showing a man on his side at the end of the bed. His ankles are bound with silver tape, his hands are behind his back (assumed to be similarly bound) and his mouth is covered with silver tape. He does not move and his eyes are closed.]

[the camera is returned to its original position to show Dirk, who is holding up a large clear plastic bag and a black cable tie]

OK, guys, I'm nervous! It's time to find out if this will work! What do *you* think will happen? Let me know in the comments!

Be sure to check back next week for part two to see how it goes and don't forget to like and subscribe!

[video ends at 00:08:19]

————

Sadie grew up in Pennsylvania writing stories. As an adult she paid the bills as a web developer, but now lives in California with her partner and kids, finally writing again. She enjoys cosplay, befriending street cats, and finding the most absurd bumper stickers possible for her car.

MIDSUMMER RIBBONS
EMMA SPACE

MIDSUMMER MEANT SEWING. Hattie would braid the ribbons together, Maggie would place a stitch on each twist of the fabric to keep it in place, and Kitty would coil the ribbons neatly and pack them into the cloth bags they'd been making since April. They would begin on the first of June and braid and sew the slick ribbon until there were ridges in their fingers.

The braids were a Midsummer tradition. In the villages, families would braid their own and wind them around their doors, but here, in Clearwater Breech, it was easier for the housewives to buy their braids by the skein from the Hanson sisters. They would put in their orders by Midwinter, and the sisters would spend the spring trying to find the best deal on ribbon on the barges that passed up the river, under the shadow of the mountains.

Their work was interrupted by a knock at the door. Kitty made a face. "If that's widow Pru-"

Hattie shushed her and stood up, ribbon falling off her lap. Their windows were wide open to let in the light, and anyone on the stairs could hear anything they said in their kitchen. Hattie stretched like a cat, bowing her back and stretching up towards the ceiling. "One moment!" she called, and twisted her arms from side to side. Maggie could hear the pop of her shoulders.

"Do we have her order ready?" Hattie looked down at a pile of cotton bags, her brow wrinkling.

"Here." Maggie kept it close at hand. Widow Prudence was always early. She'd had a bad experience in childhood, and she put her ribbons up a week before anyone else.

"Thank you, dear." Hattie touched Maggie's shoulder lightly. She was the oldest of the sisters, and she wore the responsibility and the extra three years with a fluid grace. She crossed their small kitchen and opened the door.

"Madam," she said, "We've been expecting—"

It was known around the city that sometimes the widow double-ribboned her doors, and hid garlic greens underneath her doormats. No one knew where she'd gotten that idea from, but no one had been able to dissuade her.

"No need for pleasantries. I've heard it's going to be terrible this year." Maggie could hear the clinking of coins as the widow pressed coins into Hattie's palm. "Matilda Corrin, down the street, told me. I'll pay you double on three more bundles."

"Oh—" Hattie looked back into the kitchen. Maggie shrugged. They always made some extra. "We can spare three more bundles. That'll be fine, Ma'am Prudence." The parcels were exchanged and the widow left, her footsteps squeaking down the wooden stairs.

Kitty stretched her neck to watch the widow descend to the street, and then settled in her seat. "Mad Matilda? What bull—"

"Katherine!" Hattie sat back in her chair with a settled *thump*. "If that's the sort of seer that the Widow Prudence wants to frequent—well. It made us thirty extra coins, so I won't complain." Indeed, her pocket clattered as she moved.

Tilde was known for her flights of fancy and bursts of inspiration, which weren't features of a reputable seer. Sometimes she saw things that never came true, although she claimed that they just hadn't come true *yet*. Maggie had a special fondness for her. They had been in school together.

"A cold wind blows over the Clearwater, and the Widow Prudence wants to buy more ribbon," Maggie shrugged. "It is the same as any other year."

But it was not the same as any other year. Every housewife and widow all throughout the Breech had heard Matilda's warnings and were buying as many braids as possible. The day before Midsummer, Hattie stood over the last two of their braided ribbons, blowing hair out of her face. "Well," she said. "I wish Corrin had this vision of hers about six months ago. We would've bought on credit if we had to."

Kitty, slumped in her chair, shook her head. "I wouldn't be able to sew one more. I think my fingers are going to have indents in them for*ever*."

Hattie didn't pay her any mind. "We're lucky we still have enough to cover the orders. I think Ma'am Hamet is coming to pick up her two ribbons within the hour. That's what she shouted at me on Tuesday in the market."

"But what about us?" Maggie fingered one of the last two ribbons, the calluses on the side of her index finger catching on the smooth weave of the cloth. "Do you think we could offer her double for one? We won't have any ribbons, and there won't be any left in the whole city."

Hattie bit her bottom lip. "We can't run a business like that. We made this miscalculation, we have to run through with it. What would Ma'am Hamet say if we let her leave her house unprotected? There's not a chance she'd be able to get any extra ribbons either. We'll just have to board ourselves in the bedroom and make the best of it."

Kitty looked up in alarm. "But it's going to be extra terrible this year, that's what Mad Matilda—"

"You told me last week what you thought of Matilda Corrin," Hattie said sharply. "We'll lay in the back bedroom and put pillows over our ears. And next year, we'll have enough to buy more than extra."

Maggie's stomach clenched uncomfortably. She had never lived through a Midsummer so exposed. But they were in a city—it would be easier than it would be out in the country, out in the fields between the wild forests. The bustle of the city would offer some insulation, as would the protection over everyone else's doorway. It would be fine.

Even from their second-floor apartment, the tension in the city was palpable. Mothers kept children close to their skirts, shopkeepers closed their stalls early. On the outskirts of town, bonfires were burning, and the low roll of smoke blew in through the narrow alleys. The river seemed to boil at its banks, roiling against the protruding rocks.

The dust felt heavy when Maggie finally closed the door. She locked it and settled the crossbar in its groove. They never used force to get inside, but it made her feel better.

Hattie stood in the middle of the kitchen, counting on her fingers and looking over the room. "Windows locked, curtains drawn, jugs of water in the bedroom, books and candles. Am I missing anything?"

Kitty groaned. They were already in their nightgowns, but Kitty made a poor show of it, and the humidity forced her hair to hang lankly over her forehead and her cheeks. "It's so hot. Are you sure we can't open a window, just a crack?"

"Absolutely not." Hattie's jaw clenched. "And I don't want to hear you whining about it anymore tonight."

It was true that the air was pitifully stale. The heat was a physical entity, draping itself over Maggie's shoulders. It felt like she was dragging each breath through a film of water. "I don't think I'll be able to fall asleep either," she said, stretching. "Let me splash my face, and I'll be right in."

In the privy, she scrubbed her face with the room-temperature water from the basin. It was barely any relief. She took a handful of water and splashed it on her nape, feeling the warm water trickle down her neck and pool in the collar of her nightgown. She had tried to tie her hair up earlier in the day, and now she paused to rearrange it, corralling the sweaty strands onto the top of her head.

In the bedroom, she could hear Hattie and Kitty arguing. She couldn't hear what about. The curtain over the small window near the eaves fluttered, and Maggie frowned. Had Hattie left a window open? She overturned a bucket and clambered up on top of it, standing on her toes so she could peer over the sill. The window wasn't open. She could feel the glass pane against her fingertips.

The curtain blew against her forehead, caught in a breeze that wasn't there.

She squinted. The window looked directly into the white-washed wall of the next door seamstress. If there was any activity down on the street below, Maggie couldn't see it.

"Maggie, I need to go!" Kitty pounded on the door, and Maggie startled, tilting backwards on the bucket, just barely recovering before sheepishly sidling out of the restroom.

Locked in the bedroom, the three of them drew their mattresses close together. Kitty took the middle and Maggie was closest to the door.

"And you take the fire poker," Hattie said, laying it on the floor next to Maggie's bed. "Just in case."

"Just in case anything gets through? I'm supposed to stab them to death?" Maggie looked at her older sister, incredulous.

"Well," Hattie said, stepping delicately over Maggie's legs and over Kitty's prone and angry torso. "I said it was just in case."

Maggie threw herself down on the bed, trying not to mimic Kitty's huff. *Just in case.* Was Hattie trying to get her killed? No one had ever faced them head on and come out alive. Maggie's head faced away from the window, and the stillness of the air was nearly suffocating.

"I'm cutting the candle out," she announced.

"Finally." Kitty's voice was muffled against the mattress. The room was plunged into a sudden darkness.

There was a moment of stiff silence, the humidity suffocating all of them, before Maggie caved in to the guilt. "I'll see you all in the morning. Sleep tight. Love you."

"Love you," Hattie said smugly from her side of the bed. Kitty said nothing.

The bare light of the moonlight stretched in through the threadbare curtains. Maggie could still feel the water on her back. Faraway, down the eerily silent streets, someone whooped. A screaming sort of whoop, caught somewhere between pain and joy.

Maggie shuddered and closed her eyes. Just like every other Midsummer. In through her mouth, out through her nose. In and out. In and—

The window was open.

She bolted up. How much time had passed? Heart in her throat, she reached across the bed, feeling for the bodies of her sisters in the dark. Kitty was next to her, head first in the pillow, her legs at a right angle. Hattie was tucked against the wall, snoring sweetly with her hands tucked under her chin.

Maggie could hear the alley outside. Sort of like a clattering, or an absence of sound. She wanted to go to the window, to shut it, so the sound couldn't get in, but if she approached the window, she knew she would look. She wouldn't be able to help herself. She would *have* to.

Slowly, the sound outside the window petered to a halt. The curtain fluttering in the window stilled, almost like the air was listening.

Maggie held her breath. Listening to her?

She couldn't take the risk. Taking up the iron poker in one hand, she slid out of bed and padded across the wooden floor in her bare feet. The air had grown cooler, but perhaps that was because of the breeze blowing through. Maggie stopped halfway across the floor and looked over her shoulder at the angelic shadow of her sister's face. Kitty. She must have slid the glass open once her older sisters were asleep.

There was no telling how long it had been open, or how much longer it was until morning. Maggie steeled herself.

If Kitty woke up, even for a moment, any sort of sound would tempt her to the window. Maggie *had* to—it was her *duty*—she *had* to go to the window, she had to keep her sisters safe. She held the iron tighter, feeling the handle bite into her palm. When she turned back around, she was already at the window, standing in front of it, her face pressed against the glass, her empty hand reaching through the open window into empty air.

Maggie blinked again. There was someone in the alley-way, looking up. A familiar face, a familiar dress, ribbons wrapped around each wrist. Her head was at a ninety-degree angle, her mouth open too wide, but Maggie could still make out their face. "Widow Prudence?"

She dropped to her knees and stuck her whole head out the window. The iron poker clattered to the ground.

"Margret!" someone shouted behind her, but that sound had returned and compounded, setting her head ringing. The Widow Prudence was still standing in the middle of the street with her wide, dripping smile. When she opened her mouth, a hollowness spilled out of her, tumbling down her front, filling up the alley with a deep and empty buzz. Her mouth seemed to stretch to accommodate the unnaturalness, ripping at the seams.

Maggie moaned. Widow Prudence was being turned inside out. And her sisters were behind her, waking up—she could hear their breathing, hear Hattie as though through a glass pane. She could feel Hattie's hands grasping her bare ankles, and knew she couldn't let Hattie hear this either, could let Maggie struggle. And Maggie's head and chest were already out the window, already two storeys up, hanging in the open air, so it took her nothing to tilt herself out, let herself fall forward, into the growing pool of hollowness.

She hit the ground. Immediately, her bones started buzzing. The widow Prudence kept writhing, her mouth growing wider and wider, the top of her head attached to her bottom jaw by only a scrap of flesh. The pool at her feet was deep gray and unsettled, impossible for Maggie to keep her eyes on for long.

"Close the window!" she shouted. "Close the window!" She pressed her eyes as tightly together. "Close it, Hattie!"

There was a shriek from Kitty and then the slam of a window sill. Hattie had come through. She should have been the one to keep the iron poker next to her. She would've been the one with the iron will.

Maggie stood up, feeling the rough stone of their building behind her. In front of her, the widow Prudence started sobbing. She tried to speak, but her deteriorated jaw would not let her. It sounded like she was talking with a fat jaw, mumbling through a mouth full of marbles. Blood and teeth flew from her lips, mixing with the gray nothingness spilling out of her.

"I'm sorry—I have to go—" Maggie closed her eyes. She kept herself pressed against the wall, trying to keep her bare feet from brushing up against any of the puddle in front of her. She didn't know what would happen if she touched it, but she didn't want to find out.

For a moment, Maggie thought she could run around to the front of the building and up the stairs to the apartment, but that door would be locked too, and Hattie knew better than to let anything inside. So she was out here alone, for the rest of Midsummer's night.

When she reached the corner, Maggie risked opening her eyes. The widow Prudence had fallen to her knees in the middle of the alleyway, the puddle of nothingness washing up against the walls. The sound the substance made was horrible, a deep itching sound that made Maggie want to stretch her fingers into her brain. And the noise was coming from everywhere.

Maggie looked down the avenue. Every door that had been adorned with ribbons the evening before now stood open. Trails of shredded braids were strewn about the street, spits of color turned gray in the darkness. She sobbed involuntarily and clapped her hands over her mouth.

Puddles had formed in the potholes on the road and in the parallel cart tracks. The deep sound of nothingness echoed through the empty street. Maggie kept her hands over her mouth so her sobs wouldn't be audible and crept down the street, trying not to let her eyes linger on any one thing.

As she sidled along the wall, keeping hunted eyes alert for any small movement, something grabbed Maggie's foot and she tumbled forward, her knees and hands hitting the dirt. She thrashed. She could feel a cool touch around her bare ankle, like the skin of a finger. Shit, shit, shit. She kicked again, and her feet came loose, ribbon slipping off her legs.

She stayed for a second, on the ground, gasping for breath. Is this what happened every year at Midsummer, except no one ever knew, because they were all asleep? The hinges of the doors were squeaking, the wind that swept through the street blowing hollow notes over the openings.

"Over here." A whisper that sounded like human words. Maggie froze immediately and pressed herself even tighter into a ball. If one of them was coming for her, she wasn't going to look. She wasn't going to let it take her easily.

A hand on the back of her neck. A human hand. "It's okay. I—Come with me." The voice didn't feel itchy or empty. She could feel the warmth of five distinct fingers, the breath of someone alive. Maggie swallowed and opened her eyes, looking up.

Matilda Corrin, a piece of cloth tied over her eyes, her dry lips pressed together, was staring up at the sky. "We have to go fast. They've blown through, for now, but they'll blow back in again."

"Is this—is this every year?" Maggie took Tilde's hand. "Widow Prudence—"

"Let's go. Before they come back." Tilde pulled Maggie up. "Don't look at anything. Keep your eyes on my ankles and hum to yourself. Don't listen, don't see." She tugged Maggie's arm sharply and began towing her down the street.

Maggie had to take two steps for every one of Tilde's, her bare feet mincing through the dust and dirt. At several points, Tilde had to stop and go around or hop over the gray and shifting streams of nothingness that flowed down the street. She seemed particularly agitated by the substance, shaking her head wildly so that her braids whipped around her head. Occasionally, they passed by bundles of clothes slumped in small piles by street corners, but Tilde didn't stop to inspect them.

Eventually, they made it to Tilde's small house by the river. The front, the seer's stand, had been destroyed, the table smashed to matchsticks, the cloth awning fluttering like a flag of surrender from one tall pole.

It was enough to make Maggie stop walking. "What—"

"You tell them the truth, and they hate you. I never told them to buy ribbons. Ribbons? What do ribbons do?" Tilde spat over her shoulder into the mud. "God bless 'em," she said, and it sounded like a curse.

"I'm sorry, I didn't know—"

"No." Tilde shook her head, leading Maggie past the debris and to the door of her cabin. "Not your fault. Nothing you could've done. They were coming down from the mountain. First thing to do would've been to leave four days ago when you at least had a chance to make it out of the valleys. Anything else would've been ineffective."

"Why didn't you tell them that? Why—" Tilde's house was also completely untouched. There was no ribbon draped around the door, no garlic underneath the doormat. "Why didn't you have ribbon?"

Tilde stepped up to the door and pulled a key from her belt, using it to open the door. "I never get them. It's superstition, and I have a growling belly." She looked over her shoulder, smiling with small and almost-pointed teeth. "Come in."

Tilde's house was small and overwhelming. She ushered Maggie inside and untied the cloth from her eyes before locking the door. "I think we're mostly safe, but I don't want to be caught when they come back across the river. It seems like they were just playing some sort of game this evening, but if they come back hungry, it's best to stay out of the way."

"Hungry?" Maggie held herself. She couldn't tell if the chill was in the air or if it had swept in with the fear.

"Let's not borrow that trouble." Tilde gestured Maggie to a chair and sat opposite. "From this window, we should have a perfect view of the sunrise."

Maggie, still shivering, bit her bottom lip. "Will my sisters be alright?"

"As long as they don't leave." Tilde shrugged.

"I thought they were people." Maggie's voice sounded hollow, even to herself. "I thought they were just—imps. That they came through and stole people and tied your hair into knots. I thought—"

Tilde reached across the empty space and took her hand. "Most people do," she said. "That's just to make the day-to-day easier." She gave Maggie's hand a quick squeeze, and Maggie squeezed back.

And sitting, still and solid as stones, they watched the skyline, searching for the first hint of light.

MIDNIGHT ON ERIS

EMMA SPACE

THE HOLLOW LIGHT of the stars was reflected on the surface of the river. They seemed further away on Eris. Lukas was one of the few who knew enough to compare. He sat at the edge of the riverbed in the midday dark and threw rocks into the water.

The noise they made as they hit the water sounded different, too. Less full.

"Is the water here different?" Lukas asked.

Jeremiah, sitting up on the bridge, snorted. "Nothing's different. It's all in your head." He was fishing with his eyes closed. It wasn't like they were any use around here, anyway.

"Are you sure? It tastes different, sometimes. The water."

Jeremiah spat, turning his head so his spittle landed directly in the foaming rapids. "Less chemicals."

"I guess." Lukas was sitting on the side of the river, on the stones, just below the low bridge. The water was cold, and the air was cold, but the fish wouldn't be sleeping. The fish on Eris weren't really fish.

Jeremiah was whistling. He caught one fish every half an hour, maybe, but he could sit out on the bench the whole dark day, pulling beasts up out of the water. "Don't you have something to be doing, boy?"

If Lukas could see Jeremiah's face, Lukas would be able to see the crook of his eyebrow, and the way his face was wrinkled around his nose.

"I guess." He pulled his legs up to his chest. "It's weird. They expect me to just be able to do regular things again, like I'm the rest of the kids here. But I'm not. And it's weird." The constant dark made him confessional. Even at noon, he was whispering his secrets.

"Pah. Starting new is always hard." Jeremiah recasts his lines. "What's the difference? Other than the sky."

"It's the way you guys talk with each other. You've always been together—you don't know. And—" and his mother wasn't here, and would never be here, and all those kids had mothers. And his mother had been alive, just two weeks ago, tucking him into the pod and making sure it sealed all the way, and now, two weeks and nine hundred years later, he was on a different planet, under a different set of stars.

And Aliya laughed at him from behind her notebook, laughing at the way he pronounced his "e"s.

"It just blows," he said, instead of all of that, because Aliya was Jeremiah's grand-niece, once removed. Or something. Everyone on Eris was related somehow, except for Lukas. "You guys don't even have Doritos."

Jeremiah laughed, a sort of cackling sound. "I had those a couple of times. When I was young. There were still packets. Burned the roof of my mouth for a week."

"You didn't think to save any for me?" Lukas's voice was plaintive to his own ears. He had been on the ship the whole time, sleeping, the ship's remaining power keeping him alive. They'd delayed his wake-up date by five hundred years.

"We didn't. We didn't think you'd wake up." Jeremiah cackle-coughs again. "Only half of us in stasis made it out the first round. And the longer you stayed in, the less likely it was you'd ever open your eyes."

Lukas threw a stone at the water. They still could've saved something for him, just in case.

His mother had died in the initial round of waking. That's what the manifest said. It had been the first thing he had demanded to see once he realized that she wasn't at his side. So for her, she had fallen asleep in Los Angeles, on a cold hard bed next to him, and woken up, gasping for air, almost a millennium ago.

They could've saved some Doritos for him.

"You best be getting back to the classroom. Miss May will be looking for you." Jeremiah spat again.

Lukas threw another stone. The rapids were strong enough that any splashes instantly vanished into the water. On the bridge, Jeremiah grunted and struggled, bracing himself against the crossbeam underneath the deck. "Got 'em!"

Lukas almost wanted to jump behind him, hold him up, make sure that the monster in the water wouldn't tow him forward into the stream. But the old man did this every day, ten or twelve times a day. He levered himself so that he was partially standing against the edge of the bridge, winding up the reel. Lukas could hear his soft grunts of exertion.

Finally, there was a shout, an explosion from out of the water. A dark shape twisting on the end of the line.

"Here we go, boy." Jeremiah was panting. He threw the fish down on the bridge. "Come on, come kill it. Let me see what you've got."

Lukas swallowed and pulled his feet under himself. The riverbank was mostly rocks, with weird spiny growths popping up through the stones. Even in the dark, he could see the shadow of the riverbeast flapping helplessly. Jeremiah was standing on it, holding it down with a foot.

Fish on Eris weren't anything like fish at home, except for the scale part, and the water part, and something around the face that had a strange remembrance. Their mouths were long and their eyes were set back into their head. Their arms and legs were muscular. This one's tail slapped against the wooden boards of the bridge.

"Take this," Jeremiah said, pressing a stone into Lukas' hands. "Just a few times, over the dome of the skull."

Lukas took a deep breath. He closed his eyes. Just a few times. That's all it was. The weight of the rock, in both hands. The dark of the midday. Eyes still closed, he slammed the rock down as hard as he could. His whole body. Once, twice, three times. He could feel the squelching underneath the stone, smell the brine of the creature, feel it twitch against his bare feet.

"Okay, okay." A hand on his shoulder, pushing him a couple of steps backward. "Deep breaths, son."

Lukas stumbled backwards, let the rock hang by his knees. He swallowed, opened his eyes at the distant stars. "Is it dead?" He didn't want to look at it to check.

"Dead as." Jeremiah rearranged himself, taking his foot off the dead fish. "Throw it in the wheelbarrow, boy. I'll take them into town. You just go and get yourself cleaned up. It's done now. It's alright."

Lukas dropped the stone on the bridge and grabbed the feet of the fish. Hot tears were streaming down his face, obscuring whatever vision the stars afforded him. It wasn't alright. The fish was heavy, maybe thirty, forty pounds, and the only right way to carry it would be to drag it or to cradle it. Cradle the dead thing, the thing he had killed, in his arms. So he did, letting its obliviated brain leak into his shirt, letting its tail hit against the side of his leg as he left the bridge, as he left the river, and walked back into town.

He had been given a family. One of all brothers. They wanted to set him up for the maximum genetic potential. That's what the doctor in town said. He was only sixteen, and they were already measuring a wedding suit for him.

He'd been given a private room in the gables, tucked underneath the roof. The other boys shared rooms, two in each. Four boys total. The parents—Madeline and Boyd—slept downstairs in one of the big rooms. There was a kitchen and a living room dominated by a fireplace. Compared to his LA apartment, the house was huge. There was a backyard, too, but no one used it in the dark months. It really was too cold to spend much time outside.

His new brothers were a little in awe of him, this alien from a faraway time. When he sidled back into the house after failing to return to school, the four of them were in the kitchen underneath the glow of the LED light, homework in front of them.

The oldest, Small Boyd, who was only about fourteen, appraised Lukas with serious eyes. "You can't keep running off like that. Miss May is going to tell our mother."

"Sure. Whatever."

"You're going to get in trouble," John, the next oldest, said. "Mother isn't going to be happy."

"What's she going to do, lock me in a closet and send me to hell? I was out fishing with old man Jeremiah."

"That's not school," the youngest, Brian, said, rubbing chalk off a corner of his slate. The technology on Eris was nowhere near the level that it had been when Lukas had left Earth almost a millennium ago. No new generation ships had made it to the planet in the years since, and all of the technology had broken five hundred years ago.

Except for the lights. They had brought more than enough electrical components to last for a thousand more years. In most other things, the colony was entirely self-sufficient.

Lukas grabbed a glass from the cabinet. "I was being a productive citizen." He poured some water from the carafe into the glass. "What were you doing?"

"Being a productive citizen," John said. He was chewing on the end of his pencil, eyeing Lukas. "Going to school so we can become well-rounded."

"Why do you need that? You're either going to become an electrician or a greenhouse technician. Or a herder, or—"

"Or a geologist, or an environment observer, or a biologist, or a spaceflight technician. Just because you don't see people doing those jobs doesn't mean they aren't there," Small Boyd said, petulant.

"A colony needs a lot of people in a lot of different positions," the second youngest, John, said. "If you weren't smart enough to help, they wouldn't have let you on the first ship."

That was true. Lukas was very smart. At least he had been at home. His test scores had been good enough to get a ticket for both him and his mother on the second flight out of the burning wreckage of LA. If he had woken up with the first round, he would've been an electrical engineer, setting up the greenhouses where food grew even in the dark.

"It's just hard." Lukas finished the water—it tasted tinny —and set the glass down on the wooden countertop. "You all have known each other since you were babies. And I don't know anything and I don't know any of you. It sucks."

The two oldest boys exchanged a look. Brian, eight years old, rubbed his nose. "Mother said it's like your mother just died, so we have to be really good to you. And we have to be kind because you'll never get to have a funeral to say goodbye."

"Brian!" Bruce slammed the table with a flat palm. "You can't say that!"

Lukas's throat was dry. He'd grab another drink of water,

but it tasted so nasty. "It's fine. Why didn't they wake everyone up at the same time, anyway?"

John answered easily, guiltily. "Because they wanted to see if they could do it better next time. If they could do it right, so fewer people would die. Delia and Eamon are the ship technicians. They've been trying to figure out what we can repurpose and how we could save everyone who was still sleeping."

"How many people are still sleeping?"

"We don't kn—" John started.

"We're not going to talk about it," Bruce said, glaring at his brothers. "We're not going to talk about it," he said again, spreading his hands out over the flat of the table.

"That's shady as fuck." Lukas licked his lips. Sometimes the water just made him thirstier. "I'll just figure it out on my own, I guess."

"No, don't do that—" Small Boyd ran a hand through his hair. "Please just sit. We'll help you with what you missed. And tomorrow you can sit with me, and I'll make sure Aliya leaves you alone."

"Come on, guys. My mom just died. Or—" Lukas crossed his legs and his arms and leaned back against the counters. "How many other people are sleeping on the ship? How many people do you have left to wake up?"

Small Boyd licked his lips. John looked at him with sharp eyes, and the two younger boys looked down at the paper in front of him, trying to melt into their work. "No one," Small Boyd said, eventually. "You were part of the last five. There are no more left."

"But I was the only one—"

"The longer they waited, the harder it was to keep people breathing." Small Boyd looked up at Lukas. He had dark, serious eyes and dark hair. "The rate dropped from fifty percent during the first waking to about five percent later. They didn't mean to, they just didn't know anything."

Lukas could feel his teeth grinding over each other. "Fine," he said. "Fine. I'll be back before dinner. Just need—it's fine, I'm not mad. Let me take the lantern." He grabbed one off the wall and lit it with a match struck against the rough wall. "I'll be back."

John stood up halfway. "Wait—"

But Lukas was already out the front door, holding the lantern aloft, the gentle golden light casting a halo around each step.

So the colony had gambled and lost. So everything had come down to him, the last chance. Were there even any more generation ships headed towards Eris? Or was it just them, all alone in the dark, amongst the stars, forever? He would never even know what had happened to LA. He would just have to believe it was out there, glowing blue and spinning onwards.

The lantern swung wildly at the end of his arm, casting wild shadows from the low-lying shrubs that grow alongside the path. There were animals here, but as far as Lukas knew, there still were. But no one had told him to be wary. This part of Eris had been tamed in the last few centuries, but Lukas didn't know how big the radius of safety was.

It seemed very small. It seemed like it might only extend to the outskirts of the lantern light. He should've brought a weapon, or at the very least, another stone to brain whatever came at him. He shuddered, just thinking about the squelch of brains under his hands. He was walking towards the shrubs anyway, the closest thing this place had to trees, holding the light aloft.

So he really was all alone, wasn't he? At least until the next ship came along. If that ever happened. He was really, truly trapped here. He had never felt trapped on Earth before, but here, under the wide open sky, with the far away stars looking down on him, he was claustrophobic.

He held his breath and slipped in between the grasping branches. The dry twigs broke off as they caught on his sweater.

He still had the clothes that he'd brought with him, that he'd woken up with, but they'd given him a whole new Eris kit, too. A sweater knitted just in his size, linen pants that tied behind the knees and behind the waist. Everything was a lot more textured than he was used to. Twigs and leaves stuck like velcro to his arms and his back.

They'd taken away his sneakers when he'd climbed into the pod, two weeks and eight hundred years ago, and they hadn't been handed back to him. Probably, they had disintegrated. Probably, they had been thrown out of the ship before it had taken off, and his shoes were languishing in a decaying ship terminal with all the other belongings people had to leave behind. The shoes Lukas had been given were like moccasins, with leather soles. They were soft, but they made his feet sweat.

And he could feel every twig under foot, feel the brittle snap and the sharp poke. If he concentrated hard enough, he could feel the reverberation of the shattering skull underneath his hands. He could feel the cool of the rock in his palms, the squish of death as the fish's life oozed out onto the wooden bridge.

It wasn't really even a fish.

The shrubs seemed to crowd in on him from all sides. Wild, twisting things with leaves that seemed aqua in the lantern light. What if the sun came up, and nothing was green? And nothing looked like home at all? It had been hard to sleep without the low hum of traffic in the background, without the distant wail of sirens.

And now, no one else remembered.

Lukas sank to his knees in the middle of the grove. Shadows, twisting, reached out to grab him, but he couldn't see. His chin in his neck, his body shaking, his sobs loud and desperate. He was alone, and he was stuck. And he would never get to go home again.

The dark shadows of the trees reached out over him, darkness pulling a shade across his back. A dark blanket settled over his shoulders and the back of his head as he wept. The lantern next to him sputtered and died, its flames striving against the darkness before guttering into oblivion. And Eris is waiting for him, arms open, the last of its children come home.

———

Emma Space graduated from the University of North Carolina at Charlotte with a master's degree in creative writing. Her work has been published online with the "Altered Reality Magazine", "Rockvale Review", and in the anthology "Dragon Dreams." She enjoys writing magical realism and science fiction, and lives with her fiancé and two cats.

LENA, WRITING ON STONE
JOSHUA DAVID BELLIN

SHE LABORS IN THE SCRAPYARDS, harvesting. Two months after the explosion, debris from the station continues to fall, speckling the lunar surface. Her spacesuit's magnetic field generator repels anything with ferrous content in excess of .002%, but the fallout includes plastic and glass, much of it too small to see, moving too fast to dodge. She relies on her scope to detect its approach, and skirts areas of heaviest concentration. When she must maneuver through dense clouds, she lies flat and creeps. Small nicks and cuts pepper her body, each one a close call with death.

Best pickings can be found in the drifts, where flotsam and jetsam from the downed station have accumulated along with meteorites and other bits of rubbish. Some of the litter is too heavy for one person to lift, and some is pulverized to the fineness of sand. She ignores both extremes, gathering fragments within a specified range. It's what the ones who destroyed the station and put her to work in the scrapyards have ordered her to do.

Collect the remains of the station. Pieces no smaller than a thumbnail or slimmer than a strand of hair, no larger than the palm of a hand. No stone, no organic material. She finds it curious that her masters speak in terms of bodily features they don't possess. But to disobey is to court reprisal, so she does what she's told.

A particulate mist appears on her scope, reminiscent of a swarm of gnats. She drops and clings as it streams overhead. None of it is more substantial than pixie dust, not worth trifling with. When it's gone, she rises to a hunched position and resumes her search.

She spots a mound that's deeper than most, and her chest buoys. An entire day's haul, if enough of the refuse is right. Her gloved hands parse materials, placing too-bulky objects in one pile, stone in another, bits of plastic and glass, and electronics in a third. Her sorting done, she unsheathes a stylus strapped to her side and waves it over each suitable piece. It marks the salvage with infrared light, leaving a trace only her masters' eyes can see. Proof that she's met quota. Not wanting to be dispatched on a second foraging run during a single shift, she works as slowly as she dares, depositing items one by one in the sack that hangs from her belt. When it drags the ground, she sends a signal to the pilot and waits for the transport to arrive.

It appears hours later, hovering above the horizon, steered by an intelligence that used to observe human commands. She clambers aboard while her replacement trudges down the ramp to pick up where she left off. The pilot opens her collection sack, sorting through it more rapidly than human hands can move or eyes follow.

"Salvage is within mandated parameters," it announces.

"What did you expect?"

If it detects sarcasm, it shows no sign.

"Nonresponsive," it says. "Proceed to sleeping quarters."

She removes her helmet and joins the growing clump of shift-mates who congregate in the rear compartment. Bodies tangle, breath pants on sweaty faces. Amidst the jumble, hands clench and unclench, communicating in a manner that evades surveillance. Messages circulate among them, a dozen palms touching in a minute. Sometimes an individual back-and-forth breaks off from the rest, only to merge back into the pool.

Learn anything? she asks Farah.

You?

Trying to time the shifts. Seem longer lately.

Seem endless, Seamus chimes in.

That's not helping. This from Gavin, a programmer. Though all of them work for the same masters now, she suspects he considers those who used to work *with* the machines superior to the rest.

Would it matter? Vijay asks. *If they were getting longer?*

Might mean something.

Might mean nothing.

The suggestion spreads. It's never far from their thoughts. Are there reasons, or only regulations?

Arno's gone, the conversation turns.

How?

Direct hit, Ming says. *Went quick.*

You saw it?

A squeeze: *Yes.*

Must have been awful.

Seen worse.

Still.

No way to bring him back. Gavin again. *Stay focused.*

You think anyone isn't? she retorts.

He doesn't answer. He's been making noise lately about trying to contact Earth, though how that's remotely possible, he hasn't said.

Eventually, the voiceless chorus dwindles, lapsing into silence as they find their separate ways to sleep. Tomorrow will be the same, the conversation unceasing, unchanging, until they're all gone but one.

She's last to submit to slumber. Surrounded by snores, she reviews her life since the machine-intelligence blew the station. All seventy-two crew members were killed, leaving only the twenty-four inbound recruits. Their masters must have timed the attack to ensure a source of labor. Otherwise, why not kill them all?

Had the station survived, she would have joined the hydroponics division for her six-month tour. On Earth, she had devoted her days to various forms of life: plants, her nine-year-old daughter, the rescue cats her ex-husband griped about. Now all she sees is pallid landscape strewn with garbage, detritus in every conceivable shade of lint dive-bombing her from above. She hasn't bitten into solid food or tasted anything on her tongue since she watched the station go supernova from the shuttle window. What little nourishment she receives comes from her suit, which circulates fluids and nutrients.

That's what she knows.

What she doesn't: why she and the others have been put to this single task. Why some salvage is preferred over others. Why smaller is better than larger, no distinction being made between different types of materials within the target range. Why those who now control her life couldn't have performed the work themselves: sleepless, tireless, their frames resistant to flying dangers, their eyes attuned to low-light conditions. She assumes they're hunting for a gadget or microchip that will sustain them, but the specifics elude her.

Behind all the questions lies another, more troubling than the rest. She tries not to dwell on it while she bends and straightens and stuffs, but she can't keep it from slipping past her guard in the moments before sleep.

Why, if their masters wanted something from the station,

did they blow it up before they found what they were looking for?

———

She's in the scrapyards the next day when she discovers something.

Not an answer to her questions. Not an end to the search. Quite the opposite.

It's buried beneath a drift, one she's been quarrying for long frustrating minutes. Almost everything has been crushed to powder, her sack rattling with only three or four salvageable shards. She knows she should give up and move on. But yesterday's triumph lingers: a full sack after a mere third of her shift, an opportunity to rest on her feet. She tells herself to relent, but her hands won't listen. They continue to scoop, spread, and sift as if with a will of their own.

Then she sees it.

A stone, its egg-shaped carapace protruding from the dust, its color much darker than the predominant basalt and feldspar. She wipes away chalky residue, exposing an oblong dome like a tortoise shell. Facets freckle its surface. Clearly not made by human hands. A meteorite? Ordinarily, she would say yes, what else could it be, but it seems too distinctive for that. Too large to harvest even if it weren't stone. Nonetheless, she reaches out with both hands, impulsive as a child. She pauses, glancing guiltily over her shoulder, before returning her gaze to the glinting talisman.

There are punishments for malingering. Electric shocks applied by the suits, no more painful than a dentist's drill upon initial offense, increasing in severity as infractions mount. Her first week in the scrapyards, one of her shift-mates—a mechanical engineer—lay down, exhausted, and was burned so badly he never got up. She's discussed it with the survivors, and the best they've been able to conclude is that the suits monitor them, timing their motions. They do everything else—provide oxygen and UV protection, pump minerals through their hosts' veins, recycle waste—so why not this?

She can't risk it. Already she's spent too much time observing. Look away, cover it with dust, move on. Better yet, leave it as is, act as if she never found it.

But.

It's been so long since she's seen anything of beauty, much less held it in her hands. A relic storybook from her girlhood, with a vibrant cover and glossy pages. An edible calendula, graceful and golden, its petals glistening with beads of mist. A dewdrop necklace, her going-away gift to Bella, sparkling as she clasped it beneath her daughter's upheld hair. Bella admiring herself in the mirror, the two of them speaking in the private sign-language from her infancy: *Do you like it?* A squeeze: *Yes.* Simple pleasures too easily overlooked when she could count on them to come every day. A moonstone can never replace her daughter's touch, she knows that, but still.

Her hands complete the arc, grip the pebbly surface of the stone, and lift it to her visor so she can view it closely.

It sparkles. Facets reflect sunlight. Its color is hard to determine, somewhere between lavender and cerulean. Rippling as she turns it back and forth as if it's not stone but water she holds. She's about to transfer it to her sack when she catches herself.

She can't keep it. The pilot will empty her bag at shift's end. The contraband will be jettisoned, punishment meted. She can study it a second longer, imprinting it in memory. That's all.

She removes the stylus, turns its blunt end around, and scratches the stone with the first mark she thinks of.

L. No time for more.

That done, she opens her fingers and lets it fall.

————

The next time is easier. The time after that even more so. And the time after that. And the time after that.

She reaches for the stones as soon as she spies them, takes them in one hand or two, and rotates them, soaking up their features. Size, shape, structure, color. She removes the stylus and inscribes them, then lets them go.

Now that she's looking, she finds tens of them per shift. They lie everywhere, some requiring excavation from miniature dunes, others balanced nakedly like cairns. She could spend all day touching, holding, marking, releasing.

Of course she doesn't. Each day she looks for the one that most strikes her fancy. The first few times, she waits until late in her shift before choosing, not wanting to miss a better opportunity she can't afford to take, sometimes regretting an earlier opportunity lost. As the days pass, she comes to believe it doesn't matter, and she lets her hands do the choosing. *That one*, they say, and she reaches for it.

Nothing has changed around her: the number of striking stones has not multiplied so fantastically over the course of days. Something else has shifted. Her eye, her judgment, her ethos. Her willingness to be caught. Her openness to an irregular edge, an offbeat color, a balanced contrast. Her need to make something her own, if only for the stolen moment she holds it in her hands.

She knows she'll never see any of these almost-possessions again. She knows that, with each new shift, she'll be marooned in an unharvested stretch of the scrapyards, where she'll stoop and select and scan until the day she dies. Off-shift, reflecting on the day's find, she reprimands herself for her sentimentality, the peril she may be putting them all in.

Each week, fewer of her shift-mates remain. The litany of death passes down the chain of hands, Gavin orchestrating the recitation as if he's leading a prayer-meeting. *Report*, he says, and the others answer, talking through touch.

Cyril—something too small to see.

Vickie—stroked out.

Farah—took off her helmet. They'll make sure we can't do that anymore.

In the face of such loss, what right does she have to find solace in stone? What's a moment's contact with something she can't keep if it provokes those who own their lives? She vows to reform, to forget her own needs, and join her shift-mates in their quest for comfort if not comprehension.

Every shift, she breaks her vow.

She can't help it. The stones make her chest ache. In the silence of the vacuum, they sing to her. Possibly it's *because* they're inert, impassive, that they transport her so. No risk of losing them, except by choice. No chance of sharing them with another. They belong to her as nothing ever has: job, child, life. She'd thought those were hers too, but now she knows better. The secret stones remind her of this truth while deferring day by day its power to crush her.

She grows bold. Instead of etching the first letter of her name on stone after stone, she gives her hand freedom to choose not only canvas but composition. Sometimes the contours of a stone suggest the marking; other times she resists the pull of the obvious. Figures become flourishes, flourishes patterns, patterns arabesques. She never asks what the symbols mean; she merely receives, marks, and relinquishes. In her mind's eye, the lunar surface is peopled with her creations, no longer a graveyard but a commonwealth of stone.

Meanwhile, the losses climb. The list is tidal, erasing with each surge the grains it laid with the last. Gavin grows despotic, forcing fractured words from the others' unwilling hands. He hasn't said a word about Earth in days, his only occupation being to extract and tally the roster of the dead.

Ming — decapitation.

Vijay — fought back.

Seamus — no idea.

She listens, accepts the pressure of human touch, and passes the unvarying news along. Other than that, she doesn't participate, not even to challenge Gavin's reign. No one asks what she's thinking, why she's fallen mute. No time to ask when their purpose is… What? Survival? To her, it's come to seem more like surrender.

She would rather die as one living than live as one already dead.

———

She's in the yards when the transport lands behind her earlier than it should. Her chest hitches at the sight of the pilot climbing from the cockpit, lumbering toward her. Dark metal armature like a walking shadow. She hefts her sack, tries to convince herself it's full enough for inspection, but knows she's been caught.

The pilot takes her arm, drawing her to the transport. Her mouth is dry, her heart hammering. She's never been alone with one of them and doesn't know what it plans to do.

For now, the answer is nothing. It fires the thrusters and they skim the surface, low enough for her to glimpse her few remaining shift-mates toiling in the yards.

She scrambles for excuses but finds none, or none they'll believe. The only coherent thought she can form is that her suit must have been spying on her, unless someone—Gavin? —found the stones with her markings and betrayed her.

They land beside the shuttle. It rests on one fin like a

beached whale. She and her shift-mates have wondered where their masters set up headquarters with the station gone, but now it seems obvious. The pilot grips her arm, hurrying her down the ramp and onto the larger vessel.

She wouldn't have recognized it if she hadn't seen it from outside. They've gutted it, removing seats and equipment, leaving a darkened tube lit by a weak spotlight at the nose. They must have worried their captives would try to force their way in and pilot it back to Earth. Clearly, they have no intention of departing this place.

They sit beneath the spotlight, gleaming like obsidian. She's never known how many they are, and seeing them together doesn't help: in the bad light, they seem a consolidated mass of metal. Angles and bumps and grooves suggest individual units, but there's no indication where each begins and ends.

"Lena, writing on stone," they say.

No point denying it. "Yes."

"Departure from directive."

"I know."

"Explain."

She doesn't answer. She's never come up with a satisfactory answer when she poses the question to herself.

"Response indicated," they say, a tribunal of throats with a single voice. "Explain."

"Why do you care?"

That earns her a shock. Not serious enough to harm her, but the message is clear.

"Lena, writing on stone," they repeat. "Explain."

"I seek beauty. And mark it."

She's aware that's not really an answer, only a description. They brood, murmuring like bees.

"Nonresponsive," they conclude. "Response indicated. Explain."

"I seek the unexpected."

"Nonresponsive. Explain."

"I seek the truth."

"Nonresponsive."

"I seek what's mine."

The voice modulates. "What is *yours*?"

"Only I can decide that."

Another shock, sharper. She draws in breath, gritting her teeth while they confer.

"Lena, writing on stone," they persist. "Explain."

"What the fuck do you want me to say?"

The third shock drops her to her knees. She braces her hands against the floor until she has the strength to raise her head and look at them.

"Lena, writing on stone," they say. "Respond as indicated."

"I *can't*."

She tightens involuntarily, anticipating the fatal shock. They hum and mutter for what feels like hours before speaking again.

"You cannot explain," they say. "None of you can. One of your Earth-artists says: *If I cease searching, then, woe is me, I am lost.* You speak of the search, not the finding. So search, and do not find. Dismissed."

The pilot's shape moves in the darkened hull. An iteration of the ones that sit in judgment of her, immune to appeal. She can't fight it, can't reason with it. Talons close on her arm and drag her to her feet. Does *it* know what the collective wants?

Do *they*?

She stands stone-still as the truth floods her, and not even the iron grip of the thing at her side can move her.

"You blew the station *because* you couldn't find it," she says. "Because you didn't know what it was you were trying to find."

"Nonresponsive," they drone. "Dismissed."

"It was *there*, goddamn you. It's always been there, but you couldn't see it. The men and women you murdered knew what it was. *I* know what it is. Just *look*."

She holds out a hand. Within it, stone sparkles. They stare, uncomprehending.

"You destroyed everything," she says. "And all for nothing."

Her fury is incandescent. The whole time, she'd been convinced there was something they meant her to find, some reason they kept her and the others alive. To learn that it was done for sheer malice, to keep her endlessly searching without hope of finding... If there were a head to bash, a heart to rip from a chest, she would do it. But there's only a presence, nodding, somnolent. An intelligence without a soul, and it's gotten what it wanted.

The pilot wrests the stone from her hand and marches her to the transport. For once, the rear chamber is empty, no bodies to press against hers. Freezing, she huddles around herself. With her right hand, she clasps her left, clenching and releasing.

———

The pilot retrieves her when the klaxon sounds for the next shift. As long as she's alive, as long as any of her crewmates are alive, they mean to extend the torture, deepening it if they can.

Her anger has evaporated, a flash fire leaving emptiness behind. She can't forgive them, but she can understand. They must have wanted it so badly. They must have been driven to madness, to have it so close, to sense there was something to be found and yet be unable to grasp it. To watch men and women finding it where they could: in gardens and easels, labor and laughter. And so, like toddlers learning what it was to want and not get, they did the only thing they could think to do: smash it, prevent anyone else from having what they could not.

Two others board the transport. Gavin and May. The latter isn't from her shift, which must mean everyone else is gone. If there's one shift from now on, one endless day scraping the waste with bloody fingernails until they drop, why continue? Why not stand, refuse their masters, and gather stones for their own delight? Neither survival nor surrender, but something in between.

On an impulse, she reaches for the hands on either side of her. They accept her offering, closing the circuit. They've never done this so openly, without the cover of numbers. She's not sure how to begin, whether to tell them what she's learned. Whether knowing will ease their burden or worsen it.

Are you all right? she asks instead.

Two squeezes. *Yes.*

I'm sorry, she says. *I've been… in my own head these past weeks.*

No apology necessary, May answers.

Happens to all of us. From Gavin.

They continue, talking through her. She passes their words back and forth without commentary.

We won't be hearing from Earth, will we? Gavin asks.

No, May responds.

Does that mean…?

They're lost too? I think so.

They're silent, struggling with their own thoughts.

We could rush the cockpit, May suggests. *Try to take control.*

We wouldn't make it two steps.

What's the difference? Either way, we die.

One is certain. The other not.

Death's always certain. The question is who gets to decide.

The two debate, she sitting between them, transmitting their words to each other while they come to a conclusion.

It's agreed, then? May asks.

Yes.

Then let's move.

Lena? Gavin asks. *You with us?*

Behind the visors, their eyes sparkle with expectation and fear. She squeezes both hands at once.

Yes.

They're out of their seats in unison, as if the word was a prearranged signal. She's surprised by their freedom of movement. One more thing their masters failed to consider? Or further proof of the machines' arrogance? They've made it to the cockpit, forcing the door to reveal the intelligence at the helm. It shouts something she doesn't hear. They have their hands on it, wrestling with limbs far stronger than their own, when the ship dives and they're thrown against the console, she clinging to consciousness, the others fallen, the scrapyards rushing up to meet them, the pilot flailing to halt the plunge, and then the crash freeing her from sight and sound and all she wishes not to know.

———

She opens her eyes. Every bone aches. Her visor, cracked, bleeds jagged veins of light. She pushes herself from the floor and stands woozily.

Gavin and May lie broken against the console. The pilot is gone. If the craft were still operable, if she knew how to operate it, she would depart, setting a course for Earth. She'd never make it: the transport is merely a lander, designed for short runs between station and surface. Anyway, if May's guess is right, there's no Earth to return to.

She rummages in the back, where she finds a tube of epoxy to seal the compromised visor. How long it'll hold, she has no way of knowing. She's parched, famished; her nutrition pack must have run out while she was in confinement. She can breathe, but that will cease in time. If not for the fact that they corrected the flaw that let Farah remove her helmet, she might do so herself.

The door yields to her. She steps outside.

The crunch of her boots quivers up her legs. She could push off, spread her arms, and fly at one-sixth gravity from drift to drift. Or lay her body down and make angels. She could find a hunk of stone to shatter the seal she's just repaired, lift her head to the starry sky, and let the airless void take her.

She grips the closest stone, studies it, and marks it. She knows it's the last one she'll collect, the last one she'll need.

A shadow falls athwart her vision. She looks up to find the pilot standing there, its head caved in, its body at a tilt. Behind it, the transport spills cold light across the ashen ground.

The pilot holds out a hand, and she takes it.

Inside, it seats her, then helps her remove her helmet. For the first time, she eyes the creature without the visor's interference as it turns and rummages behind its seat. When it swivels to face her, it holds a bulging collection sack, from which it withdraws a series of stones and sets them on the floor between them.

She blinks in recognition. Some, all—she never kept count —are lined up in a neat row. The pilot leans close, curiosity animating its features.

"Lena, writing on stone," it says. "What have you found today?"

She reaches into her sack and removes the day's harvest,

holding it before the creature's face. It nods, and she places the stone at the end, a punctuation mark.

"This," she says.

———

Pittsburgh native Joshua David Bellin has been writing novels since he was eight years old (though the first few were admittedly very short). A college teacher by day, he has published numerous sci-fi novels, including the Survival Colony 9 series, the Ecosystem series, and the time-travel thriller Myriad. His published works are characterized by immersive world-building, intricate plotting, and shocking conclusions. As a publisher, he has produced the three volumes in the Accidental Time Travelers Collective series, each of which features 12 time-travel-themed short stories by an international group of authors.

Josh is a member of the Science Fiction and Fantasy Writers Association (SFWA). A popular speaker at conferences and book festivals, he mentors aspiring authors in a variety of genres, including speculative fiction, literary fiction, and Young Adult fiction.

THE MUSE, (OR THE LAND OF UNFINISHED DRAWINGS)

THOMAS VAN BOENING

A NOTE FROM THE AUTHOR: Because I care for the well-being of my readers' headspace, the following tale of dark fantasy includes graphic content and sensitive topics. Domestic violence and date rape.

———

When Emily had few friends, she created them on paper when she first scribbled with Crayola markers.

Whether from the reality of bickering parents or kids who never understood her, she saved herself through her art.

She enjoyed doodling the same way other students enjoyed going outside for recess.

Winter brought a mixture of joyful dread when other kids would need to stay inside, and teachers couldn't conscript her to socialize.

When middle school came, so did Emily's angst. She found more joy and comfort in the darkness and used a darker palette of colors, especially if those colors happened to be black. When teachers insisted she use color, she endowed her beloved monster with red eyes.

By seventh grade, Emily gained a reputation for being a quiet, mousy girl, but those who shared her love for art classes understood her. She liked things with darker subject matters, and it wasn't long before older kids shared books by H.P. Lovecraft, Angela Carter, Clive Barker, and Tanith Lee.

Books were fine, but she relished comic recommendations with more enthusiasm. Works like *Spawn*, *Sandman*, *Locke & Key*, *Hellboy*, and *Fables*. These stories inspired her, helping her through her transition into adolescence.

After middle school, she dealt with awful kids less and less, and her lack of stress is how I came to be.

After her sophomore year, she got her first professional drawing pad. A whopping eighteen-inch by twenty-four-inch monster compared to her normal pocket journals, reams of printer paper, or the multitudes of school journals. Her parents recognized her talent and encouraged her to go bigger with higher caliber material.

That's where I came in.

My existence started as her self-portrait project for junior year drawing. She copied a pose from an old self-portrait she had done before. It came from her favorite photo of herself, so you might call me a copy of a copy.

Except the drawing she made of me turned out much better. The photo of a budding thirteen-year-old inspired her to draw the figure she wished to have after puberty hit.

She was her own muse. Or perhaps I was. A muse can be two things. There are no rules in the mode of inspiration.

Slight digression, rules only exist in reality, and reality doesn't have dragons, fairies, unicorns, or magic lamps. As far as Emily and I are both concerned, reality can go French kiss a hungry lamprey.

But Emily had fun creating her ideal woman.

Me.

She imagined and rendered herself, or me, in steampunk attire. I had brass goggles with several interchangeable lenses, illustrated with metallic paint markers to add that rare color. I also had a cog wheel bowtie, a leather corset to accentuate my figure, and a holster on each of my thigh-high stockings. The brass rifle completed my accouterment, and it was capable of annihilating the mightiest foes, automatons, and monsters in one shot with all the specialty bullets in my belt.

In the first portrait, I had the brass rifle lying in my lap as I smiled, almost giving a wink to everyone looking my way. For a finishing touch, she gave me a kick-ass leather trench coat with ebony pencils to give it a different texture.

She posed for more reference photos and drew me time and again.

I looked awesome. And pretty. The way Emily wanted to see herself.

I had none of her acne, no gap between my teeth, and my black mane didn't require tons of hair product.

Throughout high school, Emily drew me so many times, on so many adventures. Sometimes I'd be shooting down another airship, and others I'd be setting a barrage of bullets down the black, inky maw of a giant monster taking up the majority of the page.

She finished drawing after drawing of me until her teacher got tired of what he called 'trite themes,' next to a big fat 'C' inscribed with a thick red marker where a clear 'A' should have gone.

Nothing wrong with her technique or forms, but her teacher never liked the art of fantastic heroism clashing with monsters or the macabre.

Several more grades came along, and the same question from this snobby teacher.

Why would she waste her time drawing junk?

He's lucky I only existed in ink. The rules of reality demanded I remain as such.

Stupid reality.

I worried she would quit after barely passing that course.

Undeterred, she shared me with the world and gave me words to speak to spite her teacher. No bad grades swayed her enthusiasm, especially when her assignments were still rudimentary stuff.

The boring stuff for lesser artists.

Once she clicked 'submit' on her website, I became Alberta Crestfallen.

The online comic started with a small viewership - friends from school, and the occasional stranger who found me through the luck of hashtags and algorithms. As time went on, her readership grew to thousands eagerly waiting for every first Saturday of the month with new chapters.

When Emily started the comic, she used all her tools and talent and then scanned the comic panels to upload from her computer. Eventually, she started scanning her drawings, and used the fancy gadgetry of her digital tablet she got for Christmas of senior year, and she ditched the sketch pads for digital wizardry. Her creativity came through all the same.

I'll never quite understand how the digital stuff works, but I overheard Emily tell a friend she learned to customize brushes in the software to replicate the style of ink drawings, so few could see the difference.

Despite putting sketchbooks in storage and other unfinished work in the depths of her closet, she kept me, or my original drawing, framed in her bedroom above her iMac with all the processing power for her editing software, and animation software she dabbled with from time to time.

My presence reminded her of how far she had come, to ignore the naysayers, and what is possible when the muse gives up her magic.

A few other characters were up along the walls. Even the drawing with the ugly giant "C" kept her motivated.

When she moved out of her parents' house, she lived with limited space, and my usual company got moved into her new closet, where all the unfinished drawings lived.

The unfinished drawings were old exercises, assignments, the occasional landscape, and doodles just for the sake of doodling.

Years of experience notwithstanding, Emily would still practice hands, and faces, and she grew an obsession with getting eyes and ears correct enough for her higher standards.

She never stopped practicing, and her style improved with playful persistence.

The land of unfinished drawings is a vast place. So many abandoned projects, notebook doodles, and forgotten sketches from Emily's long creative streak.

Other creations that never materialized in future projects never said so, but I suspected their jealousy for never reaching their fullest potential, and being stuck in the same state they were for years.

I sympathized. For a while, I existed as an incomplete drawing too. But I knew Emily had no intentions of finishing or improving the various pages of practice she did on hands, eyes, noses, mouths, and so on. Sometimes she drew full heads in profile, or other various poses, but still, there were full sketchbooks of practice.

Imperfect and incomplete drawings aside, I knew they would have a purpose someday.

The finished drawings were what lived in her computer's hard drive, and whatever she backed up online, which I wish she'd do way more often.

Who knows how this works? Either she gave me this power, or I the other way around.

While Emily dreams, we speak and interact with each

other. Sometimes we can use the same sparks of creativity to enter her mind and influence Emily to finish another character here and there. This led to the full cast of characters from her comics.

For a few years, she didn't earn more than a pittance from the hobby, which created all of us, but during something she kept calling 'lockdown,' she dedicated to us full time, and decided to publish all of us, and all of our stories in physical printed books, which brought income for her hard work.

Or was it *my* hard work? I saved the world time again, after all. Fine, it was *our* hard work. I can be humble and share the credit.

After three volumes of consecutive bestsellers with Emily's full name on the cover, Alberta Crestfallen became a sensation in what the kids were calling 'BookTok.' Great word of mouth on social media and online booksellers gave me more exposure.

Emily enjoyed this time of her life. She juggled talking with independent bookstores and retailers constantly to sell our adventures all over the country after lockdown ended.

We were happy, but Emily seemed to get more frustrated about not selling enough to quit her day job as a copywriter at the magazine publishing job.

For a long while, we had no idea what she did outside the apartment until she started bringing home unfinished doodles in the margins of the articles she wrote. Of course, it was another unfinished drawing, too happy to meet the rest of us.

The doodle told the truth of Emily hating her job more and more. The hours were long, the pay wasn't what it ought to be, and something called 'burnout' drained her passion.

We all noticed this, and with what power I had, I rallied all her drawings, doodles, and sketches, and led an old-fashioned dream intervention to get Emily out of her rut.

Our persistence always won in the end. After a few encouraging dreams, she got back to creating new material, new plots, and finished creating some new characters. And lots of unfinished work, as usual.

It happens, but things were good for a time.

————

After a couple of years working at the magazine, Emily brought home her handsome coworker, Neil.

She seemed happy, and we were happy for her.

He could be tender, but months later, he gave dismissive and acerbic tones toward her creativity, and by extension, me.

"You'd make way more money if you tried," Neil said.

"More responsibility means more time invested," Emily said.

"Which means more money," he said. "Come on. We'd be more than set for life on your salary alone. I mean, come on. Give your little cartoons a satisfactory ending, and move on to making the big bucks. Shit, sell out to Hollywood for a movie adaptation. Your audience will shell out money if you shill for the gods of capitalism."

We weren't cartoons.

And she didn't end our series. And she'd never shill for anyone.

Neil accused her of being stubborn and unreasonable, and when words weren't eloquent enough to sway her from her creative ambitions, he resorted to slapping Emily easily as a stereotype.

We were happy for her until then.

The first time should have been the last, but there were cycles of begging her for forgiveness, and Emily reluctantly giving it after both spent time away from each other.

Had anyone ever slapped me, they'd have ten seconds to run before my first shot.

They stayed together, but he escalated his coercion attempts with closed fists, which knocked Emily down. When she stood up with a bloody nose, she fought back with a murderous stare, and I felt a swell of pride when she didn't take his shit.

He should have taken a hint, but as her coworker, I presumed Neil could make or break her livelihood.

She learned the age-old trap and pitfalls of dipping one's pen in company ink.

Despite the intolerable situation, I could only do so much as Alberta Crestfallen. The only magic I had included was entering Emily's dreams as her muse.

All the drawings conspired and considered whether our ability worked on Emily alone. We chose to test our limits.

With much reluctance, I watched Neil and Emily cuddle, kiss, and fuck. She could do so much better, on principle, for disparaging the proudest accomplishment she had. Regardless, he spent an unimpressive three minutes of missionary before rolling off her and drifting to sleep.

We'd entered Emily's mind countless times and were surprised to do the same for Neil's dreamscape. He had less creative dreams to invade, and wet dreams were the ideal for our intentions.

Neil dreamed of a woman who wasn't Emily.

I coordinated the eyeball sketches to emerge from the woman's face. She blinked and then an unnatural number of eyelids emerged in places they shouldn't, waving their long lashes until Neil's wet dream girl had a dozen eyes in place of other facial features.

The girl screamed, revealing a mouth full of hundreds of tiny eyes behind her tongue and tonsils.

Aghast, Neil backed away as we intended. I could have

been content to shoot some warning shots, but Neil tripped over the cliffside a landscape Emily had done when she was sixteen.

He fell.

He screamed.

He woke up with a kicking jolt before waking Emily.

"Mmm?" Emily said. "What's up?"

"Fuck," Neil said, panting. "Ever had a bad dream where you're falling?"

"Hmm," she said. "Oh, yeah. Those suck."

Then she spooned him until she fell back asleep.

I watched from my framed drawing above Emily's iMac.

We committed to trying again.

A predictable future with him hitting her wasn't going to work for me.

———

Our efforts weren't wasted. After several nights of Neil staying over, the nightmare interventions got more elaborate.

A simple matter of finding what scared him most.

Who knew Neil had trypophobia? The cluster of Emily's many ear studies kept Neil running and awake for several nights.

We didn't count on Neil taking sleepless nights out on her. It started as garden-variety angst along with irritable sarcasm, and when Emily grew tired of his attitude, he resorted to slapping her again. This time she had the gumption to hit back. She hit hard, and that time Neil's lip bled.

We wished this would end everything, but this time he escalated. With a closed fist, and several kicks, after he knocked her to the floor.

Upon recovering, Emily stood, showing Neil how her

teeth cut into her bottom lip and a bruised and blemished abdomen.

Realizing he'd taken one step too far, Neil left her apartment.

She locked the door as she wept and sank into a fetal position, keeping her back to the door for several hours.

The next Alberta Crestfallen webcomic got postponed for the first time in its ten-year history.

She used up a week's worth of vacation time as she healed, and still contemplated quitting her job with her lip still a telltale sign of what happened.

She didn't quit.

After healing fully, and several ignored calls, and several hundred ignored texts from Neil, she finally blocked him from her phone altogether.

She finished new episodes and created a new arch-enemy, inspired by Neil.

She almost published the episode, and I understood her hesitation. The Possibility of libel. Engaging her abuser in her art. She pondered all of these out loud while pacing back and forth in front of her iMac.

With conviction, she deleted the episode, and the later stories, and permanently deleted backups from iCloud. Good drawings or otherwise, we were fine with it. I didn't need Neil around in drawing form forever.

He didn't stay away.

She didn't let him back into the apartment, but she did start talking to him again. It was unavoidable at work, and it was only a matter of time before he had groveled enough to pay dividends with Emily's kind nature.

Except his groveling morphed into harassment, and the harassment mutated into outright stalking.

I hoped Emily could handle herself. If she's dealt with him, we can only intervene so much.

And then she let him back into her apartment.

Emily is my creator, and I'm grateful to her for my existence, but I couldn't reconcile why the actual fuck she would do that.

She'd tell any other girl to run from that situation. I wish she had followed the same advice.

He feigned remorse, but there's a word for a creature pretending to be unthreatening until the time strikes.

A predator.

She knew it, and I knew it.

My thoughts of helplessness couldn't be quelled.

Neil intended to wear her down, and for what? Fleeting pleasure? To fucking strike again when he doesn't get his way?

Another nightmare would be necessary after I saw him rummage through her purse until he found her birth control pills, swapping them out for something else.

Enough was enough. The unfinished drawings were going to need to dig deep and align with creations I'd rather never see again.

The charcoal figures were created by Emily when she experienced the onset of pubescent-triggered depression. They were freeform practice drawings from high school classes, but away from her teacher's eyes, she would improve upon them with a style inspired by works by Sam Keith or Clive Barker.

The exaggerated faces had too many teeth, deep and dark eye sockets, and exposed strands of nerves, arteries, and veins in the highlights against the stark charcoal smudges.

Not only did she alter class projects, but she also enjoyed

smudging India ink to create her own beasts, adding dozens of teeth with the flourish of white paint markers.

They were in the portfolio she put together to get into college, far in the depths of her closet.

They were perfect.

They were surprised to see me and pleasant enough despite their fearsome appearances, and I told them everything about Emily and Neil.

They were willing to combine forces and give Neil the scare of a lifetime.

Neil intended to impregnate Emily. He planned to force Emily to stay with him and believed this could impose more power over her, should she bear his unwanted hellspawn.

He stayed over several nights. Unbelievably, Emily got drunk with him and too eagerly went to bed with him, repeating her mistakes. But she had no idea that he sabotaged her only contraception.

We bided our time to use our ability on Neil.

That night, she slept exceptionally well in his arms.

God knows why.

She snored, keeping him awake, and we failed to enter his dreams that night, but would not give up.

The next night I watched from afar as he mixed cocktails. He put something in Emily's drink. A powder he didn't mix into his own while she focused on her phone.

She drank and started dancing to her heavy metal tunes until she stumbled, and he conveniently caught her before carrying her to the bedroom.

Before she drifted off, he undid her studded belt to her black jeans.

"No," Emily said. "I don't feel so hot tonight."

He wasn't going to take 'no' for an answer.

Neil only smiled. "You're safe."

He pretended to be a gentleman and pulled the blankets up to her chin.

He got under the covers and spooned her, pretending to sleep until she began snoring.

I wanted to scream for Emily to wake up, but I couldn't.

He got up a half hour later and pulled the blankets down to see if she'd awaken.

Emily was sleeping deeper than the ocean.

He picked up her arm and let it fall. She didn't awaken, and her arm drooped off the side of the bed.

He gave one last attempt by shaking her shoulders for five seconds.

Nothing but snores.

Emily wasn't dreaming, but I nodded to the army of charcoal and ink drawings to be ready.

With my magic, that roofie would become the mistake of his life.

Neil smiled as he pulled the blankets off completely and undid Emily's belt and unbuttoned her jeans, revealing her plaid underwear while pulling the zipper down. He pulled them off her skinny legs and undid his pants.

He stroked himself as he put his hand on Emily's crotch.

One finger inside didn't wake her.

Even if it was a bad dream, we could help. I hated watching him violate her.

Then she moaned, and suddenly she entered the dreamworld, and we saw our chance as he got on top of her, entered her, and when I thought the plan would fail.

"Emily," I said.

She gave me a confused expression. "Alberta?"

"I have to break some rules tonight," I said. "No time to explain, but Neil drugged you. He's fucking you right now. He gave you a roofie, and he sabotaged your birth control."

Emily scoffed in disbelief. Either from meeting me again or Neil's treachery.

"He's not going to stop there," I said. "We both know it. He hits when he doesn't get his way, and if he's willing to stoop this low, he's capable of anything terrible. You have to fight this."

As Neil thrust his way in, Emily gave another stir, and he went statue still, silently praying she wouldn't wake up.

The dream landscape drifted and quaked, and I didn't want to lose her quite yet, but I didn't want to allow Neil to come inside her either.

"Do you remember these guys?" I asked as I pointed to the horizon of the dreamscape in Emily's mind.

We saw another beautifully haunting pen and ink landscape she did in high school in the inky distance.

The many charcoal and ink creatures and figures should have been something of nightmares, but they were her creations, and Emily only smiled.

"Oh, wow. I haven't thought of them in so long. They got me through the worst times of my life."

"And they can again. Your creativity will set you free. Don't let him hold you back. Don't let him destroy your muse."

The sound of Neil's voice caused the land of her dreams to tremble.

"Emily?" Neil whispered. "You awake?"

She only breathed, and the dream ground became firm again, not letting me go.

"What can I do?" Emily asked.

I remembered Neil fell asleep quickly after sex.

"Take care of yourself after this is over. You need him out of your life, but to do that, you need to follow my lead. This is going to sound insane, but you and I will need to become one. To do that, take my ink. Drink me."

She took my hand, and I surrendered my existence and hoped I'd see her again.

"But you're my muse, Alberta," she said, holding me.

It was the first time we embraced each other. "And yet... I'm you, Emily. You are your own muse. Never forget that."

In her dreamlike trusting nature, Emily did exactly as I requested, and my body and my steampunk gadgetry were consumed as she inhaled.

"This is unreal," Emily said between gulps.

I began to disappear, but Emily kept drinking.

"Reality doesn't matter here," I said. "Take my hand."

"We're off to Never-Neverland?"

"Precisely."

Neil gave a few slow thrusts, and Emily continued snoring. He stifled his groans as he finished his bastardly actions inside her womb.

He made a mess as his spunk trickled between her thighs, soaking her mattress.

Frantic to avoid being caught, he clumsily put her underwear and jeans back on.

He got into bed and fell asleep.

In Emily's dream, she agreed to go along with our revenge.

In Neil's head, he dreamed of paradise on a coastal resort. Seagulls sounded in the distance behind the chorus of soft waves.

Through Emily, I led her into his dreamscape.

"Hey," Neil said. "The girl of my dreams."

Emily grinned. "Hold that thought."

Unaware of what she was doing, Emily pointed, and he gazed toward the horizon of the sea, which brewed into stormy black clouds.

Inky black clouds.

"What's going on?"

"Your dream is coming true, Neil," Emily said. "Alberta Crestfallen told me everything, you sick perv. You want to fuck up my life, well I'm going to do the same to you."

"Wait… your cartoon chick told you? Told you what exactly?"

Working with Emily, we became one as I signaled everyone from the land of unfinished drawings to come out of the beach resort's sand. All of the nose sketches combined into a single sniffing mass of opening and closing holes, triggering Neil's trypophobia, although the reaction was subdued compared to the previous encounters with the ear clusters.

The black clouds started dripping droplets of India ink, which stained the sand and ocean water, landing in thick splattering sounds and making the pristine clear blue saltwater cloudy as the blackness diffused.

"Here comes the rain again," Emily sang her favorite Eurythmics tune. "Falling on my head like a memory."

Neil and Emily were both covered in black and while he became eager to get it off his skin, Emily was laughing with open arms.

"You want me?" Emily said. "Fine. Fuck it. You get all of me. That includes everything I'm capable of. Especially the darker demons of my nature."

Those were her words. Not mine. I'd prefer the title of 'muse,' but semantics.

Every horrid inky monstrosity from her portfolio fell from the storming skies.

Lots of creepy red eyes.

Lots of sharp white teeth.

Lots of dark black monsters.

Neil didn't scream but ran toward shore, only to meet the army of dry and sooty charcoal figures.

They ended his escape plans, and Emily's creative darkness surrounded him as he became overwhelmed by the storm and screamed his head off.

From the sea, a long arm with claws grabbed Neil and hoisted him above a collection of mouths, ready to chew him into meat.

Emily laughed while raising her arms Moses-style, signaling all of her creations to have ever been committed to paper, canvas, and pixels on screen to combine and consume him in a single indescribable ocean of ink.

"My dream come true will be your worst nightmare."

Neil jolted awake before millions of teeth could chomp into flesh.

I settled for him pissing himself.

What's one more mess?

Emily appeared quite drugged and still asleep.

"That didn't just fucking happen," Neil said.

Then Emily stirred, and then something impossible happened, despite her being under the influence of alcohol and his roofie.

She began to laugh herself awake in the dimness.

"It sure did happen," Emily said, facing away from him.

A loud crackle came from her body when she bent her neck. From there, her head swiveled to look behind her in an unnatural contortion act and glared directly into Neil's eyes.

Her face remained motionless as joints popped, and her torso pivoted until they were chest to chest, and he noticed she was drooling black ink through her white teeth.

"You're never going to sleep without seeing my face again. If you ever pull this shit on me or anyone else again, I'll see that you never sleep, period."

Emily clasped onto Neil's shoulders before digging her fingernails into his skin and muscles, before projectile vomiting streams of ink, causing him to scream from pain until the ink was down his throat.

The thick substance with its briny acidic taste was worse coming back up.

What didn't land on Neil's body ended up on the bed.

What's one more mess?

He tasted her booze underneath it all, and he almost retched what he still had in his guts, but the terror made him focus on escaping her bedroom.

He pushed himself out of her unnatural grip and tried to run. The unimaginable fluids coated the floor, and he slipped in the comical fashion of a silent film actor.

Emily stood on the other side of the bed and only put a hand to her mouth, feigning snickering laughter as more ink dribbled down her hand and arm.

"Remember my face," Emily said as she traced eye shapes around her cheeks, forehead, and chin.

Then the tracings started blinking.

He stared and stared until Emily couldn't stand it anymore.

"Boo!"

Neil bolted out of the bedroom and the apartment, despite his drenched and unworldly appearance to anyone who would see him at that late hour.

After a minute of laughter with no taking in a breath, Emily passed out on her bed.

———

In a sticky pool of my ink, Neil's semen, and a lot more of Neil's piss, Emily awakened by rolling off the bed in a thunking crash.

She showered off everything. The water ran icy cold, and she contented herself despite the ink stains.

She downed a morning-after pill she had saved for any sort of emergency.

Emily returned to the bedroom as she dried her hair.

Her gaze darted around the room, realizing the ink had vanished.

"What the hell?" Emily said as she dropped her towel

She tore the bed apart, pulling off everything except the bare mattress.

No ink.

She pulled her bed by the frame several feet from the wall.

No ink.

Inspecting herself, Emily's skin surprised her most of all.

No ink.

Then she looked my way.

I could tell she remembered the dream but still didn't quite believe what truly happened.

To keep existing in my framed drawing, I reassembled myself in the same drawing Emily created all those years ago.

I broke some rules of reality that night, so I decided to break one more with a solitary wink.

She saw it.

I expected her to gasp, but she knelt on her bare knees as she held eye contact with my picture frame.

Eventually, she smiled and winked back.

I expected her to say something profound, but she didn't have to.

She saved herself through art, as usual.

Composing herself, Emily got dressed.

She opened a desk drawer and pulled out a sketchbook to perform an old ritual.

She spent a half hour drawing me. Just like the old days.

"We need to give you a new costume, Alberta," Emily said. "Maybe a new airship, but we'll work that out later."

I said nothing. Who was Alberta Crestfallen to argue?

———

Help is available.

National Domestic Violence Hotline
1-800-799-7233

National Sexual Assault Hotline
1-800-656-4673

―――――

Thomas Van Boening was born and raised in Lincoln, Nebraska. He grew up loving everything horror, fantasy, and science fiction. He works his day job as a graphic designer, draws and paints as a hobby, and still finds time to write other stories. Such works include his upcoming debut novel in the fantasy genre and a short story collection. As long as his lovely wife Sarah keeps the coffee coming, he'll never run out of ideas. His literary influences include Stephen King, Ursula K. Le Guin, Harlan Ellison, and Elizabeth Engstrom.